THE HOOD FLOWER GIRL

A NOVELLA

M. MONIQUE

CONTENTS

Chapter 1	1
Chapter 2	10
Chapter 3	22
Chapter 4	36
Chapter 5	50
Chapter 6	61
Chapter 7	76
Chapter 8	88
Chapter 9	100
Chapter 10	115
Chapter 11	128

Copyright 2024 © M. Monique
Published by M. Monique Presents

All rights reserved, Including the right to reproduction in whole or in part in any form. Without limiting the right under copyright reserved above, no part of this publication may be reproduced, stored in, or introduced into a retrieval system, or transmitted, in any form by means (electronic, mechanical, photocopying, recording or otherwise), without the prior written permission of the copyright owner.

This is a work of fiction. Names, characters, places, and incidents are either the product of the author's imagination or are used fictitiously, and any resemblance to the persons, living or dead, business establishments, events, or locales, is entirely coincidental.

To those still waiting for their flowers...

CHAPTER 1

MEMPHIS MCCORVEY

"Are you gonna go inside and get ready for Grandma's funeral?"

While pulling from the blunt, I ignored my little sister at first. She was in my fucking business on a day I didn't need anybody minding my fucking business. It was all I could do not to find a nigga to put my hands on. This anger and aggression inside me were begging to boil over.

"And you know Daddy doesn't like you smoking. It gives Mama a headache if she smells it."

Fuck my pops if I was being for real. Nigga needed to worry about the hoes that were going to show up today to pay his mama their respects. Meanwhile, they had no respect for the woman who birthed me. They were the reason I'd come to hate disrespectful ass women just as much as I hated disrespectful ass niggas.

"Nikki, go back inside," I told her. This blunt was getting me right. The longer she stood here, she'd blow my damn high.

"I'm not leaving until you come inside with me."

As she talked, gravel crunched beneath someone's stride. Glancing back, we both saw my closest nigga, Boston, coming up the driveway. He wore a scowl, and it was directed at Nikki.

"Go put some fuckin' clothes on!" he barked.

Nikki smacked her teeth. "Boston Kelly, I'm not one those girls you mess with for you to be talking to me like that. Mems, get yo' friend before I cuss him out."

Both Boston and I thought that was funny. Nikki wasn't the type to "cuss" out anybody. That was partly because she knew all she had to do was call her big brother, and I was coming to clear shit out.

I dapped Boston, then addressed my sister. "You do need to go put some clothes on, baby."

This time when she smacked her teeth, she stormed off with a growl.

"Bruh, I'on know how you do it. I wish my fuckin' sister would come out the house in some shit *barely coverin' her fuckin' ass*!" He yelled that last part to get Nikki's attention. Without looking back, she flicked him off and continued up the long ass driveway circling my parents' property.

"What you doin' here all dressed up anyway?" I asked him. Boston was my homie since middle school. We clicked the moment a nigga tried to bully my sister and Boston beat that nigga's ass like a drum.

"Had to come support my nigga, the fuck. Besides that, you know Nana McCorvey was my baby. I couldn't miss her day."

Her day had me fucked all the way up. I was too old to not understand that life ended. Whereas I thought my grandmother would live forever, cancer came along and proved a nigga wrong. Taking the most precious and loving part of me was like taking my damn breath. I loved no woman above my grandmother. Not even my mama, and I loved her to death. My grandmother was just…different.

"You really gon' miss the way she cussed you out every time you walked inside her house witcha shoes on?"

Boston busted out laughing, and so did I.

"Mane, I looked forward to it. Half the time, I did that shit on purpose. If she wasn't cussin' me out, my day wasn't gon' go good."

Reflecting on better times, I shook my head.

"She was supposed to see us graduate college and shit," I mumbled. "That's all she ever talked about was me and you staying out the streets."

Boston rested his hands in his pockets and casually shrugged.

"Now look at us… knee-deep in this shit."

Yep. Deeper than I wanted to be in some pussy right now. This blunt wasn't hitting like I needed it to anymore. I ashed the tip and stuffed it into my pocket.

"You think we oughta hold up her wishes for us?"

Boston's question had me deep in thought. A nigga was twenty years old and out here pushing too much weight for a nigga my age. My ass should've been in college somewhere, learning how to do chemistry or some shit. I was good at working with chemicals.

"The fuck we gon' do with a college degree besides hang it on a fuckin' wall?"

He shrugged again. "You never know. Maybe one day we'll look back and realize this dope game ain't the life for us and we'll have something to fall back on. Not that we need a degree to maneuver in this world. Money ain't a problem for us. I'm just thinking that we can honor her wishes. That's the least we can do."

"Yeah, I guess," I drawled.

Going to school would've at least pacified my mama as well. She hated the life I was in but wasn't surprised since her husband had been in the same life. All Jonathan McCorvey knew how to do was sell drugs. He dropped out of school as a teen and never looked back. Truthfully, my mama thought I would do the same thing. When I graduated with honors, she was pleased.

What did she expect when my grandmother was the best teacher in the city? Despite how my daddy disappointed his mama, I never wanted to disappoint my grandmother. Whenever I had an issue in school, I ran straight to her for help. She was my tutor, my disciplinarian, and most of all, my grandmother. I respected her so much that even when I needed to do some dirt, I kept it far away from school and her. She wasn't naïve to think that I was the golden child I presented to her. My grandmother was just hood enough to keep me in my place. As long as I respected her, she didn't have a problem.

"Shit, how the fuck am I gon' get through English without Nana?" Boston really looked concerned, so I laughed.

We were really going to miss that damn lady.

POPPI BLOOM

"They're gon' laugh at you when you go over there."

I straightened my long, denim skirt and ignored my sister, Tandy. While cackling, she followed me out of our shared room and into the garage where my work was located.

"You know doggone well the McCorvey family thinks they're better than *every*body in the city. They won't even let you make it to the front door to knock." This time Tandy laughed louder.

Shaking my head, I said, "Then I'll just leave the flowers in the driveway." As long as they made it there.

"Not only did you do them for free, but they gon' throw 'em in the trash anyway," she continued.

"Tandy, please." My sister could be so negative. We were two years apart and for whatever reason, she loved ragging on me about the dumbest things. Like me making flower arrangements.

"And another thing. Mrs. McCorvey was a mean ass English teacher. I wouldn't be makin' her no flowers."

I whipped around and glared at Tandy. "Don't talk about the dead. Are you crazy? When ghosts show up on your bed tonight, don't think you're gon' keep all the lights on and keep me from getting my sleep." Rolling my eyes, I snatched my shoes off the shoe rack and put them on. I had to hurry before my ride made it here in order to make it to the McCorvey's house before the family left for the funeral home.

Mrs. McCorvey was responsible for me graduating school early. Without her, I would've still been hanging around kids who didn't like me. Hell, I didn't like them either. Thanks to Mrs. McCorvey, I was a high school graduate at the young age of sixteen. Although I was eighteen now, I never forgot Mrs.

McCorvey. Because of her, I spent my time doing something I actually wanted to do—like playing with flowers. One day my passion would turn into big bucks. Hopefully.

"Auntie Rose is gon' be mad at you for going clear across town while she's not here."

"That's why I'm trying to leave before she gets back."

"You're weird," she mumbled before going back into the house.

Waving her off, I loaded the three flower arrangements into the wagon I'd bought just for this occasion. I made it to the bus station just in time and boarded my bus with hopes that the McCorveys wouldn't be too snooty.

Following the directions to the house tucked away in an expensive neighborhood I could only dream about living in, I came upon the house ladened with cars lining the curb and driveway. They weren't just any cars either. They had expensive names on them and were cars I'd never been so close to in real life. From the street, I could only see a glimpse of the house. Large, tall trees blocked my view.

Unsure of what to do, I started up the winding driveway. I didn't want to leave the arrangements out of view. I'd just drop them by the front door and hurry out of here before anyone saw me. My plans were dashed away when I saw the driver's side door of a luxury vehicle open. Putting my head down, I tried walking past it without the person noticing me.

"I see you, shawty," the deep voice touched with a little humor said.

"Hey," I spoke to the boy who stepped out of the luxury vehicle, smelling strongly of marijuana. The smell was so strong that I waved my hand in front of my face. It was a quick distraction from his handsome face. I wasn't particularly boy crazy, but I acknowledged when I thought a boy was fine or whatever.

Not only was he fine, though. He was built like a mammoth for someone who couldn't have been much older than me. The passenger side door opened, and another boy stepped from the car. He was just as fine and built as this boy. The first boy smirked. He had a stunning face. One that was too fine to not think about even after I left here.

"You act like yeen never smelled grass before, which I know can't be the truth. You from Ensley Heights, right?"

My eyebrows crashed together wondering how he knew that.

"Yeah, you that girl with the garden an' shit. The Hood Flower Girl. Ain't that what they call you."

"Who are you talking to, Mems?"

A girl my age came down the driveway dressed in a designer outfit that put my denim skirt, white tee shirt knotted at the belly, and white canvas shoes to shame. I wasn't what I wore, so I put on a smile.

"Why you in our business?" the other boy asked the girl.

She put her hand in his face and walked right past him to come up to me.

"I'm Poppi, one of Mrs. McCorvey's former students," I introduced myself.

The girl looked me up and down before saying, "I like that skirt."

I wasn't sure if she was trying to be funny or not, so I simply smiled.

"Who are those flowers for?" she asked.

"Mrs. McCorvey. I made her some arrangements… if that's okay with your family."

Collectively, the three assessed me from my head to my

scuffed white canvas shoes. She came even closer to me with a questioning gaze.

"Why?" she asked as her fingers played along the petals of a white daisy.

"Why what?" I muttered and popped her fingers when she nearly plucked one of the petals off.

Mems chuckled, causing the girl to glare at him. "First of all, you're still not dressed."

Mems simply shrugged his large shoulders.

"Why would you bring flowers for my grandmother?" she turned back to me and asked.

"Well," I started. "She was a sweet teacher." Mrs. McCorvey was the only teacher who acknowledged the genius in me and did something about it. The rest of my teachers seemed to have an issue with me, which stemmed from the family I came from. My family was nothing like the McCorvey family. We didn't own land, expensive cars, big houses, or any of that shit.

Laughter brought me out of my thoughts.

"*Our* grandma was sweet?" she quizzed skeptically.

I nodded with a smile. "I mean… she was sweet to me."

"Oh, you must've been the class goody two shoes," Mems said as he smirked and tilted his head.

"Among other things," I proudly stated. "I could be the class bully if anyone tried me."

To that his smirk turned into an amazing smile. I lowered my eyes because he was too fine, and I had no business looking at him like I wasn't a virgin. I was sure he'd already learned his way around a girl by the way his cockiness was set up.

"How old are you?" the girl asked.

"Eighteen next week."

"Not trying to be funny, but where did you get money to buy these flowers? They look expensive."

"She grew 'em," Mems answered for me.

He was correct. My garden wasn't one that was full of variety. For the time being, I grew only four flowers, one being daises. It took weeks to grow healthy, beautiful daises. But I had a knack for growing flowers. They were my hobby. I'd already made good money off of making flower arrangements for different people in my neighborhood.

"You *grew* these?"

I confirmed with a nod.

"Wow! They're beautiful." Her smile was comforting. What surprised me was when she took me into a long, tight hug. "You're so sweet for this." She released me and beamed down at the flowers.

"Yeah," Mems added. "You aight, I guess."

On my way home, I held a smile that no one could take away. Tandy thought I would get laughed off the McCorveys' property. Granted, I never made it *inside* the house. Instead, I left with Nikki McCorvey's number. She wanted to have lunch with me one day.

As a girl who had no friends and pretty much stayed to myself, my smile grew bigger at the heart over the "I" in Nikki's name.

That was sweet of her.

CHAPTER 2

POPPI

Four months later...

"Hood!"

Memphis's deep, cool voice snapped me out of the haze I was under. Once the fury of flames snapped, the shouts of bystanders and instigators bounced around in my brain. As if I didn't know what the hell was going on, I glanced down at my sore hand which had a wad full of this bitch's hair. My other hand rested by my side; fist balled up like I was in a heavy weight fight. By the look of my fists, I'd done damage to her face.

Good. Running her mouth got Chacha right where she needed to be.

"Bully ass bitch!" I barked and released my hold on her. Breathing heavily, she stumbled back and immediately reached up to check her face.

"It's fucked up," I confirmed for her. "Let these hoes who egged you on clean yo' shit up, bitch."

This girl had been doing too much shit to Nikki, and I wasn't having it. Nikki was the sweetest person I knew besides myself. She wasn't the fighting type, and she never liked confrontation. I was the same with the exception that I wasn't backing down from anyone. I didn't give a damn how big or intimidating my opponent seemed, I stood my fucking ground.

I let the two fight it out, until one of Chacha's girls tried to jump in. I wore her out just for Chacha to come at me too. Both of them were embarrassed and angry that "the flower girl" really had some hands. They wanted another go at me. Their friends were hyping them up to have another round. Memphis stood between us, though, and dared them to come near me.

"You got what you came here for. Nie get on," he warned the group.

Neither of them wanted to walk away the loser. However, they knew damn well not to fuck with Memphis nor Boston.

"I told y'all to wait for me to get to the school. The fuck was y'all thinkin'?" Memphis was angry, and he wasn't staring at anyone but me. "And you not even supposed to be over this way."

I glanced at Nikki, who snickered behind her hand. Although she wasn't a fighter, I was proud of her for standing up for herself. She'd done enough to make Chacha's girls feel like they had to jump in and help their friend out. Nikki's other friend, Shayna, on the other hand, looked like she wanted to cry. Her parents didn't play that fighting shit and would ground her for a while.

"I skipped class so that I could make sure they weren't gon' *try my girl. If you're always running to the rescue, people will still fuck with her. You won't be around forever."*

Matter of fact, Memphis was leaving to go to school next weekend. He didn't understand that his presence was only good when he was here. Once he left, the bullying shit would start back.

Memphis eyed me, his gaze stern and scary. In the four months I'd known him, I came to find out that Memphis wasn't the boy to fuck with. I kept referring to him as a boy when Memphis was all man. He moved like no other boy I knew. And he drove a car no other boy in the entire city drove. Not to mention, he had money…a lot of it. I wasn't naïve to think he wasn't out here dealing drugs.

"I agree with Mems. Y'all should've waited for us." Boston grilled both me and Nikki. Two months ago, I witnessed him choke a nigga simply because the nigga called Nikki a bitch. I guess I'd been around too many people who used the term so often, that I wasn't so easily offended by it.

"It's not Poppi's fault," Nikki said. "Chacha wouldn't shut up, so I told her to meet me at the park."

The park was two blocks from Nikki's school and provided a little space for scrapping. This was where most fights occurred.

"Hood knows better, though," Memphis said.

"My name is Poppi, and—"

"And I don't give a fuck. You not in high school anymore, baby. You can't be fightin' these damn girls."

"Fuck that!" I shot back. "A senior is a senior."

Boston chuckled, then stopped with a mug from Memphis. The difference between the two of them was that Memphis was more laid back than Boston. While Memphis was more *calculated with his actions, Boston got active...and quickly. I learned all this in four months.*

"I tried to stop Nikki, but she wouldn't listen," Shayna said. She was always trying to win Memphis's attention to the point it was nauseating.

"Next time, take yo' ass home," I told her. She was the type to snitch if shit got sticky. I didn't like that.

"Poppi!"

I snapped out of the memory and back to the present, recovering from my lack of focus with a smile.

"You look beautiful, Nikki!" She really did. The custom-made white, shoulder bearing, Sandra gown flowed over her curvy body like fine caramel. Behind her a five-foot train stretched and sparkled with intricately woven crystals. Those same crystals adorned the fitted bodice of the gown. My best friend looked truly stunning.

"You're looking at her like you want a piece of the pussy."

Coolly, my eyes turned to Mika. Mika was that chick that I avoided at all costs. Although she was Nikki's *other* best friend, I kept that girl at least five hundred feet from me. For the past eight years, I'd done well to stay far away from her. That wasn't so as of late. *My* best friend was getting married, which brought her circle of friends together.

"*Please*, don't start with her," Shayna groaned. She was still the same old girl who hated drama. With me and Mika sharing such close quarters, Shayna was more anxious than either of us were.

"Don't tell her anything." I wasn't going to cut up because this was Nikki's day to shop for a gown. Although every cell in my body wanted me to say something back, I swallowed my evil words with a sip of wine.

"We've been at this for three hours, so hopefully you really like this one." Qita was Nikki's closet cousin and one of the bridesmaids. She was ready to go as her nigga kept blowing up her phone.

"I do like this one."

I could tell Nikki liked it because she couldn't stop smiling. The bell over Sandra's entrance door caused Nikki's smile to slightly falter. Glancing over my shoulder, my face screwed up at Boston waltzing in here like he owned the place.

"Baby, I told you we were almost done." Shayna stood from the sofa to enter her husband's arms. She placed a kiss on his hard set, bearded cheek. That whole relationship was weird. One minute she was fawning over Memphis, the next minute, she was Boston's wife.

"Nah, you said that shit two hours ago. The fuck is takin' so long?"

Sandra's eyebrows piqued at Boston coming into her place of business with that foolish energy.

"My fault, Sandra. Shayna ain't take this long to pick out a dress." Boston pointedly looked at Nikki. "This shit ain't that damn serious."

The entire bridal party collectively gasped, including me.

"Should I call Memphis to come collect you?" I asked because no one else dared to talk to Boston like that.

He shot me a smirk. "He's outside."

My heart stopped in my chest. Just knowing Memphis was in the same vicinity as I caused my panties to quickly stick to me. Boston knew his comment shut me up, so he went back to glaring at Nikki.

"We got shit to do. Is you done or not?"

Nikki glared right back at Boston and flipped off, "Nope."

It was funny because the dress Nikki had on was *the* dress. She just wanted to fuck with Boston. It worked. He moved out of his wife's arms and stormed out of the store. Shayna giggled along with the other ladies. I watched the play of emotions on her face, seeing through the fakeness of her laughter. Then, I glanced at Nikki. Her head was down as she smoothed her fingers over her dress.

What the hell was going on?

The rest of my thoughts stopped short in my brain as the bell sounded and Memphis entered the shop. His thick lips were set in a subtle snarl, and I couldn't help but notice how fresh his lineup and beard were. Memphis had the perfect jawline, the perfect bushy eyebrows, the perfect nose… He was just a sight to behold. My panties were already clinging to me and now they seemed to disintegrate as his eyes immediately fell on me. For a second, he said nothing. He just stared.

MEMPHIS

"You're not gon' keep me from going to an event that *I* was invited to!"

A nigga really didn't do this arguing shit. The minute Daphne raised her voice, I hung the damn phone up. My sister's giggling had me glancing over my shoulder to see her coming into the study, where I'd dropped my luggage.

"She's right."

"She can be right all she wants to." I ignored the incoming call from Daphne and placed my phone on the large oak desk I rarely used but paid a fucking grip for.

"I don't have a problem with her coming."

"I do. If I want this relationship shit to die down, I gotta move without her anywhere near me."

Nikki chuckled. "It's been months, and the press is still painting you and her as a couple. I get it. But I invited her; not you."

"Why are you here again? Where's Eddie?"

"I came here to give you a piece of my mind. Do you and Boston always have to pop up and ruin shit? My day was going fine until y'all barged inside of Sandra's like some robbers."

Nikki wasn't truly mad. My sister had always been sweet and docile. Even when mad, she never raised her voice or allowed her anger to come of anything other than silence.

"Boston was lookin' for his wife," I said with a sour expression written on my face.

Nikki giggled and like that her anger dissipated. "You really think Shayna is crazy enough to ignore her husband?"

Shrugging, I replied, "Ain't my business. I was just there in case guns had to be drawn on Eddie's behalf."

She laughed. "First of all… you don't even fuck with my fiancé like that even though I keep begging you to let him in your fold. I'm surprised you've even agreed to go to his bachelor party. I know it's a little ways out but knowing you'll be there makes me happy."

I gave her a crazy ass look. "I gotta go make sure this nigga don't do some dumb shit that requires me to put a bullet in him."

Wincing, she placed her hands on her hips. "Don't lay a finger on him. Eddie's a good man."

I simply shrugged.

"You're a good man too. Which is why I don't understand why you aren't ready to settle down."

Leaning against my desk, I folded my arms over my chest and crossed my feet.

"Who said I'm not ready to settle down?"

"Uhm, all the women you discard. I thought things were good with Daphne and *surprise,* y'all aren't together anymore."

"You think you know me or somethin'?" I joked.

Nikki smiled. "I know you *too* much, bro. Like the fact that you keep running from every woman you meet simply because the one you want won't allow you access to her."

I cocked my head and assessed the knowing look on my sister's face.

"If I wanted access to Hood I could have it."

She smirked. "Who said I was talking about Poppi? And just like she wishes, I wish you'd call her Poppi and not Hood."

I only blinked.

Sighing, Nikki walked up to me and brushed some lint off my shirt.

"Stop stressin', baby girl."

"I can't. Not until you realize you're about to lose out on a good ass woman."

About to?

Nikki saw the look on my face and nodded.

"I hear that a certain local property appraiser is trying to spin the block. And he's serious this time."

"Good for him," I grated out.

Cutely, Nikki chuckled. "We both know you don't mean that."

"Again," I started. "You got all the answers. If you wanted me and Hood together, you'd be tryna vouch for a nigga."

"I've vouched you out, big bro. Poppi isn't trying to hear any of it. You gotta remember, she's watched you grow from the twenty-year-old young man you were, to the man you are now. Depending on her perception, it can be either good or bad. However, you can't blame her for how she views you."

"So, we're back to square one."

"No, we're not. You stop running… and maybe she will too. You think it's a coincidence that you broke it off with Daphne the minute you found out I was getting married?"

"I was done with her way before that," I corrected.

"But you kept fucking with her. You never truly broke it off until Eddie proposed to me. You broke it off *that night* to be exact."

I grumbled and hated the fact that she remembered that shit.

"All I'm saying is, a part of you knows you're on borrowed time with Poppi. You're going to roll over one morning with a business deal while she's being cuddled by a man who will never love her the way you do."

"That's a strong ass word, shawty."

"And yet you have strong ass feelings for my very best

friend." She stopped me from protesting. "Which is completely fine. If there's one person I'd want my brother to love for the rest of his life, it's Poppi."

I chuckled. "You stretchin' shit."

"No, I'm not," she fired back. "That's the only way you're going to get Poppi. If you come less than correct, I'll be the first person to tell her to walk away from yo' ass. As my brother, I love you, but I won't watch you fuck over my girl."

"So maybe I need to stay away from her. One fuck up and she's gon' be done with a nigga."

"What do you consider a 'fuck up', Mems? Cheating—"

"Nah, no shit like that." If I ever got my hands on Hood, I'd never do some shit like that to her. "I'm a well-known businessman, baby. You already know how shit is for niggas like me. Case in point, this shit with Daphne. How am I gon' step to Hood when the press is still spinnin' this *at best* past fuck buddy shit?"

"Create your own press."

I shook my head. "That ain't me."

"Exactly. If *you* get on the internet and—"

"I'ma have to stop you right there, baby."

"Okay, okay." She laughed. "Let me handle it. Just make sure you're ready to complete the deal."

After a few ticks, I said, "I'm ready."

Shit, I'd been ready. Hood was a contract I couldn't sign if the toughest lawyer laid her before me. She dodged a nigga at every fucking turn. Nikki hustled from the study just to return seconds later with her phone. With a big smile, her fingers flew as she typed something.

"There... and there!" She beamed with pride. "Go on IG and view the post."

"Nikki—"

Smacking her teeth, she snatched my phone up, ignored another call from Daphne, and sifted through my apps until she made it to Instagram.

"You're more active on IG than any other platform. Look," she said, putting my phone in front of my face. "People are already reacting to it. Give Poppi a minute, she will too."

Glancing at the post, I read the caption:

My brother @memsmccorvey & my fave flower girl @hoodflowergirl_poppi

The picture of me, Poppi, Nikki, and Boston was one taken on the fifth anniversary of my grandmother's death.

"How is this supposed to help me?"

Nikki smiled. "Because… look at the way you're looking at her."

Sure enough, in the picture, my eyes were on Hood. Maybe it was the way my teeth tugged at my lip, and the way my eyes said everything my usually unfiltered mouth couldn't that this moment captured. I was a young nigga in love with my first crush.

I came home from college many weekends and saw Hood often. There was something about that day that had me on her tough. Ever since, I couldn't shake my feelings toward her. I'd been playing it cool, though. At least I thought I was.

Walking into that bridal shop today and seeing her sitting there with a wine glass tilted towards her juicy ass lips did something to me. Shit, seeing or even thinking about Hood always did something to me.

"Trust me. Every woman who views this post is going to comment on how you look at her. Poppi won't comment on the way you're looking at her, but those comments will plant a seed. At this point, you need all the help you can get."

Damn if a nigga didn't wait all evening to see what Hood's response to the post would be. I wanted to break my damn phone when I saw the fucking caption she posted to her story.

Family* *heart emoji

The next morning, I got up and got right to business. As much as I wanted to obsess over Hood, I had moves to make.

CHAPTER 3

POPPI

THREE MONTHS LATER...

I groaned the second I saw Shayna walking across the yard. Per usual, she had her nose tooted up as she tried navigating the plush grass in her high heels. All I did was shake my head. As long as she'd been coming here, she hadn't learned yet to wear other shoes besides heels.

"Uh, uh!" she fussed when she saw me trying to disappear from the showroom. "You didn't respond to my text. You better be going this weekend, Pop."

"You better be glad I'm even considering it."

"Alright, alright, damn. You always gotta be so uninterested."

"I'm not uninterested. I just have other things to do."

"Like what? Work? Girl, you're gonna watch all your life pass by being in this shop."

"Which is perfectly fine, Shayna. Let's not forget you also

have a dad who owns the company you work for. Many don't have the luxury of spending our days shopping and pampering ourselves when work awaits."

She smacked her teeth and waved me off. "I don't shop every day."

I gave her a look that had her sheepishly grinning.

"All I'm saying is missing one weekend of this place isn't gonna cause you to go out of business. You *have* to come with us to Atlanta. Nikki won't enjoy her bachelorette party if you're not there. And I be damned if I spent all my hard-earned money on this trip just to not enjoy it."

As much as I loved Nikki, I really didn't want to go to her party. Not only was I swamped with orders, but I was still itching to knock the uvula out of Mika's throat. Then again, I would've been a horrible friend not to show up and support my girl, and I was always there for Nikki.

"I'm only going because I don't want to stress Nikki out, which I know the rest of y'all will do. I'll be there to offer her some peace."

Shayna shrieked with joy.

"Just ignore Mika like you have done for the past eight years. No one holds a deeper place in Nikki's heart than you."

I rolled my eyes even though it warmed my heart that Nikki loved me so much. Then again, the way she felt bothered her other friends. Shayna was the only one who seemed to understand that we could all coexist while having the same best friend. Although Shayna and I started out rocky, she'd grown on me over the years.

"The only reason you're her flower girl is because you asked to be. You could've been her maid of honor."

"Psshh. I was not about to argue over no damn spot with

Mika. I'd end up beating the brakes off her and then there wouldn't be a wedding at all."

Shayna cackled, but I found nothing funny. Mika had been friends with Nikki longer than I had. Whereas Nikki didn't let money and status make her a mean bitch, Mika let it be known that she didn't fuck with "broke" people. I found that funny since I wasn't broke. I just wasn't wealthy like them.

"Excuse me, but how much is this arrangement?"

Taking my eyes off Shayna, I glanced at the older lady standing in front of a display of my most expensive arrangements.

"Two hundred," I answered without shame.

She issued me a stank look. "I know you lyin'. This ain't even a real store and you're charging that damn much for some flowers that's gon' die."

Shayna's eyes bugged at me. She knew my mouth was reckless and sometimes, it was hard for me to censor it. Calmly, I met the woman's unpleasant brown eyes.

"Ma'am… this *is* a real store, and those flowers have an extensive shelf life."

Just because my flower shop was the house I grew up in, people really thought it was okay to play with me, my money, and my time.

"Extensive shelf life my ass. I heard you was supposed to be cheaper than the folks on the other side of town."

The folks on the other side of town charged double what I did. A floral arrangement that size would've been far more than my modest two hundred dollars.

"You're welcome to go across town and check the other floral shops."

THE HOOD FLOWER GIRL

Flo's Petals wasn't hurting for money. Even if it were, I would never beg a soul for their business. Majority of my customers were word of mouth, and I had several repeat clients. Funerals, weddings, special occasions, and fuck-ups happened every day. I was cool on money and clients.

The lady smacked her teeth and continued to peruse other arrangements. Rolling my eyes, I turned my attention back to Shayna. Now that I thought about it, a short break from this place wouldn't have been so bad. Going to Atlanta for the weekend would probably help me get out of this weird ass funk I was in.

A funk that stemmed from a picture of me and the man I'd been crushing on since I was seventeen. I couldn't get the image of Memphis out of my head. It was one thing to sit back and secretly harbor feelings for someone. It was another story to think that they sat back and harbored feelings for you too, because damn it if that picture didn't speak in volumes.

"Since I'm going to Atlanta, I'm gon' need you to get out of here so I can pull these orders together. Don't bother me anymore today."

Giggling, Shayna came around the counter to hug me before she skedaddled. Shaking my head at her, I sighed and watched the lady as she peered at my floral arrangements with her nose tooted up. She mumbled under her breath several times, then decided she was good on what she'd seen and left.

The sigh of relief I was about to let out died the minute I saw the silver luxury sedan pulling into the makeshift parking lot in front of the shop.

Jermaine got out of his car and glanced around before making his way inside.

My ex was mouth-watering sexy. His handsome dark looks

rivaled any actor appearing on a woman's wish list. He was tall with toasted brown skin, a Caesar cut, and deep ass dimples that made many women swoon. He forewent most facial hair just to make sure his dimples got the proper attention he needed. As if his corded body didn't draw attention all by itself. He knew how to wear a damn suit, that was for sure.

"You blocked me as if I'm not the type to pull up." He walked right up to me, chuckled, and tried to hug me.

I dodged it and went behind the counter to put space between us. Jermaine was good at smooth talking, which was how he swindled his way into county office.

"Don't make me take the necessary steps to make sure you no longer *pull up*. Your constituents would be flabbergasted."

His white teeth showed as he laughed. "You'd never, Poppi. Your heart is too good. Besides, as much as you want to deny it, we were good together. There was no reason for us to part ways, and yet, here we are."

"Jermaine, please. There were many reasons for us to part ways. Should I name the three women who seemed to be your favorites?"

"I can't help that you're a jealous woman, Poppi. I've never touched another woman while we were together."

I laughed in his face. This nigga really thought I was that stupid. If I showed him the pictures in my phone, Jermaine would've had a coronary.

"Lying has become so ingrained in you that you'd sit in front of a jury and feed them this same bullshit."

His face reflected the truth. He sighed and smoothed his hand over the small patch of hair on his chin.

"I want you back, aight. That's all. I'm serious this time."

"Which you said a few months ago, and I told you *then* that I wanted you to leave me the fuck alone."

Jermaine thought just because I didn't have a man, that he should've been the one to fill that void. If only he knew that he could never fill a spot that wasn't created for him. I'd told him to move around several times. He couldn't even compare to the man who truly held my heart.

He saw Nikki's car pulling in next to his and immediately winced. Meanwhile, I thought Nikki couldn't have shown up at a better time.

"Are you going to consider us?"

"Nope," I chirped as Nikki breezed into my shop. Her face was already set in a mug before her eyes landed on Jermaine.

"Hey, boo!" She came around the counter to hug me without even acknowledging Jermaine. I chuckled on the inside.

"Hey, girl. Eddie know you on this side of town?"

Even though I was kidding, she waved me off. Eddie grew up just a few blocks from here and, although he was wealthy as hell, he didn't forget his stomping grounds.

"I'm here to *force* you to take this money."

I was already shaking my head 'no'.

"I won't, Nikki. Use it to buy yourself something nice."

"I don't need anything," she fired back.

"E-hem…"

Nikki and I glanced at Jermaine whose face reflected his aggravation.

"Just talk like I'm not sitting here," he said sarcastically.

Nikki rolled her eyes so hard, Jermaine mugged her. He knew that was all he'd better do.

"You're interrupting my day, not the other way around," I replied.

His gaze swept over me before he tilted his head and retreated.

"I think you made him cry," Nikki quipped.

I smacked my teeth and covered my mouth to keep from laughing. Jermaine glanced over his shoulder as he exited the shop to see what was so funny. After the door closed behind him, Nikki rolled her eyes.

"You better not fall for his shit, Poppi, or I'm gonna be really mad at you. He's really serious and won't let up."

"Baby, please. He had his chance and he wrecked it. I'm not spinnin' the block to see if he's still standing on it."

She beamed. "Good. Because my brotherrrr—"

"Nope." I stopped her dead in her tracks.

"Poppi," she whined.

"Stop trying to make a case for Memphis. That picture you posted is *still* catching too much heat." Every time I checked my notifications, I cringed at seeing someone like or comment on that damn picture.

Yet, you look at it every chance you get. Damn myself, I did. How was I supposed to continue dodging Memphis when everyone was constantly reminding just how fucking sexy he was and how he damn near wanted to jump me in that picture.

The thing with Memphis was simple: every woman wanted him. That was a set up for heartbreak, something I'd been successful at not ever having. The closest I came to heartbreak was when my mama got sick and left me and Tandy on our Aunt Rose's door step. I was young but still able to process that my mama wasn't mentally healthy enough to care for her kids. At least she had the wherewithal to place us in good hands before she committed herself.

"Poppi, come on," she continued. "He'll do right by you, I swear."

"First of all, ma'am, you should be focused on your bachelorette party. Not me and Memphis."

She blinked at me for several beats before she dropped it. Good. I didn't need any help consuming my mind with thoughts of Memphis. He did that enough all by himself.

MEMPHIS

I yawned and stretched while working out the muscles in my back and neck. Before rising from the bed, I checked my phone to make sure I didn't miss anything throughout the night. I'd had a fat blunt and a few drinks before calling it a night. This was the first time in a long time I'd slept like a rock. My phone wasn't in my hand five minutes before it rang. I answered my sister's call without a second thought.

"'Mornin', baby. Wassup?"

"What are we gonna do about Poppi? I saw her yesterday, and that slippery ass nigga was there begging to get her back *again*," she emphasized.

I frowned up at the thought of that nigga still biting at Hood's heels.

"You should go take her out to eat or something. Just, I don't know, pop up on her ass and make her go to lunch."

"You know as well as I do that Hood ain't goin' for that shit."

Nikki made a noise that sounded like a growl. "Listen, big bro. We put the picture out there and you haven't done the first thing to capitalize on it. Why not?"

Because Hood swept that shit right under the rug. So, I did, too.

"She shared the picture and put 'family' above it. That means she ain't studyin' a nigga like you think she is."

"Mems, you're a business man who handles million-dollar deals at your leisure. Are you really gonna pretend like you can't read between the lines? Poppi is just…scared, alright. She doesn't know what to expect with you."

Glancing at the time, I saw it was too early for this shit.

"Listen, baby girl. I know you want me to move in on Hood, but at this point, I'ma leave shit be." I wasn't going to admit to her that Hood's lack of interest in me fucked me up. I could have any woman I wanted and didn't have to beg one for shit. Plus, I was a nigga who didn't let shit move me. Too much time spent obsessing over Hood had me neglecting every need I had. Throwing myself into work was one of the only ways I kept thoughts of her at bay.

Nikki scoffed. "You better not, Memphis JaDarrian McCorvey!" she hissed. "How can you know with everything in you that you're letting your soulmate just…just…"

"Slip right through my fingers?" I finished for her.

"Right! That's dumb and you know it. You make shit happen all the time. Make shit happen with Poppi."

Scrubbing my eyes, I sighed. "Why is this so concerning to you, baby?" Ever since Nikki peeped that I had a thing for Hood, she'd been on my case about having her.

This crush I had on Hood…it was heavy. Just the way she *moved* attracted me.

"Because… Grandma once told me that we should never walk away from true love. True love was what kept her comforted in nights when she was sad and hurting. Grandpa being there beside her made transitioning easy."

I gulped back my emotions from Nikki bringing up our grandma. I'd never fully dealt with her death and damn sure hated reliving how much pain she was in, in her last days.

"Do you think Ma has true love with Pops?"

Nikki was quiet for a minute. She hated talking about our parents. Where I saw every evil thing our pops did to our mama, Nikki hadn't. Most times, she learned shit through the grapevine. She stayed defending Pops when she knew deep down that he was no good. I wasn't trying to treat my woman the way he treated our mama.

"Mama has stayed all these years," was her answer.

"That's not what I asked." I stood from the bed, then went into the bathroom. I placed Nikki on speaker and put the phone on the counter while I brushed my teeth and washed my face. She was quiet through both.

"Answer me," I finally said after she still hadn't responded as I moisturized my face.

"Why would she stay with him?" Nikki's voice broke for a second.

"Nah, we ain't finna do that," I warned her. Hearing her cry would set me off.

Plenty of times, I tried talking my mama into walking away from her husband. That seemed fucked up. But it was more fucked up that the nigga couldn't keep his fucking dick in his pants. The minute I moved out of the house I grew up in, I cut my pops off. Nikki still had some ties with him while I could give a fuck about that nigga.

"I wanna say that I wish Dad would do Mama better—"

"But you know it's not in him. A man has to wanna be faithful and shit. Muhfuckas act like that shit is complicated and it ain't."

"Says the man who keeps more than one woman at a time. Daphne was the first one I thought you'd do right by, but you didn't. Which is why Poppi stays far away from you."

I started the shower and hated that she ventured back to Hood. She wouldn't leave my damn mind with Nikki bringing her up again.

"None of the women I was with were my fuckin' wife. That's a big ass difference."

"So, you intend to marry Poppi?"

"Nikki," I drawled.

"It's a valid question. I already told you, you gotta step to her correct."

My sister wasn't going to let up, so I said, "How can I know that if there's nothing there besides her callin' me *family*."

Nikki giggled. "That was messed up, huh?"

"Fucked up," I agreed.

"Well, that was then, this is now. Trust me, when I saw Jermaine yesterday, he looked like he was at the end of his rope. I'm praying Poppi doesn't fall for his shit."

"Look, I'll go see her, aight?" Just to get her off my phone line, I told Nikki what she wanted to hear. I wasn't about to step foot near Hood. I had a big contract on the table that required all my attention. Aside from Eddie's upcoming bachelor party, I was in work mode and didn't have time for anything outside of that.

Two hours later, I made up any fucking thing to stop by Hood's shop. The only time I drove through Ensley Heights was to come see Hood. While there were niggas over here getting money, they weren't my clientele. If a nigga's bread wasn't long, he couldn't fuck with me on any type of shit. Broke niggas didn't mind robbing, snitching, or killing for a dollar. I mean, everybody had to find their way to feed their family, and I wasn't knocking anyone's hustle. From the shit I'd done in my lifetime, there was no way I could judge a muthafucka.

I parked in front of Hood's shop and assessed the street line. A few kids were on their bikes, riding up the road and cussing each other out. Just up the block, a couple of women stood on the corner staring down the street at me. The cocaine white Bentley always drew attention.

Across the street, a house rundown on the outside was the

playground for a few niggas who sized me up the same way I did them. As if a bullet couldn't catch me, I gave them my back and entered Flo's Petals.

There wasn't anyone in the showroom and when Hood appeared from the back, her eyes rounded at the sight of me. Ignoring the fact that she had soil all over the white smock emblazoned with Flo's Petals, I walked up to her and hugged her.

"'Sup?"

"What are you doing here?"

"I came to pay for the flowers."

Curiously, she looked me up and down as I gave us a little space. Touching her caused my body to respond. She moved to the checkout counter with her eyes never leaving mine.

"I'm not letting you pay me for Nikki's flowers."

"You can't make me not pay you, Hood."

She glanced away for a second, and I took the chance to re-enter her space. Her eyes flew back to me with some nervous apprehension there.

"Well, either way, you could've called," she mumbled.

"And miss the chance to lay eyes on you?"

"Memphis, stop." Her oval-shaped face tinted prettily. I'd never been able to find a more beautiful woman than Hood. Those doe-shaped eyes with the slanted tips got me every single time I looked into them. The way her hair was styled into that bob was just as fire as any other hairstyle she'd worn over the years. I swear, with each passing year, she grew more beautiful.

"So, we just gon' pretend like there's no fire between us?"

Said fire danced all in her eyes. It was nothing for me to spread her open on top of this checkout counter and fuck her until she complied with every fucking thing I said.

"Just because there is doesn't mean we should stoke it."

The fact that I got her to finally admit it made my chest swell with pride. Stepping closer, I smiled at the way she visually stopped breathing and clutched the counter behind her.

"I definitely think we should stoke it. If there was ever a time I wanted to fuck a woman into submission, it would be you."

"That's what this is about? Submission?"

"Nah, my bloom." I reached out and pushed her hair behind her ear. She trembled under my fingers. "If you haven't realized it yet, I'm actually the one doing the submitting. I'm practically groveling at ya damn feet."

That brought a shy smile to her face. I wasn't sure how Hood managed to be so damn sweet and tough at the same time. Those were qualities that first made me fall for her. I loved that she was both cotton candy and Jolly Rancher.

"Niggas like you don't grovel, Memphis. How would people who're afraid of you act if they knew you were...*groveling*?"

"Fuck them," I said. "People who really know me, know how I get down. Including you."

I watched her teeth sink into her lower lip and that shit had me moving to close all the space between us. Then the bell above her door sounded, breaking the hold I had on her. Gone was the Hood who was ready to let a nigga have his way. In her place was the Hood who didn't give a damn about my ass. I had to chuckle to keep from strangling her.

CHAPTER 4

POPPI

*A FEW DAYS LATER... **Atlanta, Georgia.***

I grimaced at the way my ass looked in the ripped jeans I wore, questioning if I should change. My outfit choice was giving "streets" when I needed it to give "chic boardroom". At least for tonight.

Nikki's bachelorette dinner was starting in an hour and if I wanted to get there on time, I had to decide on a look. Rifling through my suitcase, I didn't pack anything except jeans, a couple of button downs that I could tie at the navel, and a couple of bodycon dresses. I wasn't in the mood for either of the dresses tonight.

Sighing, I just stuck to what I already had on and went into the bathroom to give my face another once over. Satisfied that I looked decent, I dimmed the light, grabbed my clutch from the bed, and headed into the living room.

"Mems outdid himself with this suite," Shayna said as she too appeared in the living room. She and I shared a suite since I didn't too much fuck with anyone else. She was decked out in a black shimmery dress that hit her at the knees. It was thin strapped and modestly covering her breasts, yet still made her look stunning.

"Okay!" I had to give her props.

"Me? Look at you showing *all* yo' skin," she teased because I rarely did that shit.

"Come on, let's go so we can meet the other ladies on time." We both moved to the front door where I slid into my designer sparkling, strappy, high-heeled sandals. My toes were painted a bright pink, which beautifully contrasted against my mahogany brown skin.

Shayna reached up to tweak the back of my hair, making sure every strand of my asymmetrical bob was in place. The deep part on the side had my bangs fluttering in my face even though I curled them backward. It was my favorite style to wear, so I didn't mind moving the strands every so often.

Shayna and I arrived at Black Waves, an upscale restaurant and club in the heart of downtown Atlanta. It was situated amongst a plethora of other clubs which irked me just a little bit. I had a feeling we would be down here all night once the liquor started flowing. We stepped out of the chauffeured sedan that Memphis provided for us and strutted up to the entrance with several pairs of eyes watching our every step. A man who looked familiar stood outside the door. I had to shake my head. I forgot that Memphis rolled this way. He didn't let his sister do too much without security. Especially when she was out of town.

Speaking of Memphis, he was here in Atlanta, too, for Eddie's bachelor party. The wedding wasn't for another three weeks. However, Nikki did a lot of shit to accommodate her brother's schedule.

While I was on the subject of Memphis, I had to admit that he surprised me. He was a businessman who made so many moves in the business world, that his and Boston's names were sure to cause other businessmen and women to shake in their boots. They weren't typical businessmen. Their dealings were, well...not all that legal. Sometimes they kept their hands clean and sometimes they didn't. I knew all this by way of Nikki. She hated that her brother and Boston wouldn't go full on legal with their ventures. However, she trusted them with everything that was in her.

A part of me wished that I could've trusted Memphis just the same. I broke code admitting to him that I felt the flames between us. Ever since, I couldn't sleep, eat, or take a piss without thinking about the way he looked like he wanted to devour me. My pussy agreed that Memphis most likely knew how to get her right.

"Good evening, ladies," the server said as he escorted us to a private room guarded by another one of Memphis's goons.

"Finally!" Nikki squealed as we walked in. The room was covered in beautiful drapery that opened to the street line. Black leather chairs flanked either side of the stately dining table. Beautiful floral arrangements drew me in as I went to hug Nikki.

"Sorry, we're a little late," I said. Then spoke to everyone else. The only person who didn't speak back was Mika. I was cool with that. As long as she didn't say shit to me, I was cool. It didn't go unnoticed that Mika sat right across from me. While she stared a hole in my face, I ignored her ass.

As I went to take my seat next to Nikki, I fingered a lush rose petal with a smile.

"Whoever did these, did an amazing job," I praised. There were five placements on the long table, each just as vibrant as the other.

"May I get you ladies something to drink?" I rattled off my choice of wine to the server and so did Shayna, who sat on the other side of Nikki. As Nikki's matron of honor, Shayna was fulfilling her duties to a T. Everything was coming together so nicely.

"I'm so glad you're here," Nikki said to me.

Although I almost didn't come, I was glad I was here too. "I'm gon' always have your back, Nikki." She smiled brightly, then looked out over the table.

"I'm thankful that y'all came on this journey with me. Soon, I'll be married and living in wedded bliss. While a couple of you know what that feels like—"

The married ladies grumbled in disagreement, causing Nikki to cackle.

"—I'm praying that everyone at this table finds love. Not just any love but true love."

Somehow Nikki's eyes found mine and stayed there.

"You know, where your person can simply look at you and cause everything inside you to turn to mush. Like no one ever existed but them."

Nikki and I held our gazes. There was something hidden there that I wanted to be nosey about. Sure, I felt like she was talking about her brother, but there was something else there too. For a woman just weeks away from her wedding, Nikki rarely talked about the shit unless we were actively engaging in activities that involved the wedding.

"Well, damn. I hope I find a man like that." Qita broke the awkwardness of the table's quietness.

Clearing her throat, Nikki dropped her eyes for a second before they were back to being bright and cheery.

"I'm gonna go to the restroom," she said as she stood. Watching her retreating back, I wondered what the hell was up with my girl. I almost followed her until the server came back with my drink. It was barely on the table before I lifted it and took a heavy sip.

"Poppi *does not* have a man. We can't count that property appraiser nigga. I think he was just a front anyway."

The only reason my ears perked up to Mika's voice was because I heard my name. She spoke lowly, but Poppi definitely left her chapped, dry ass lips.

"Excuse me. Poppi what?"

"Lord," Shayna mumbled.

Mika regarded me across the table with her nose turned up. "What?"

Her attitude really ground my skin like some beef, but I kept it cute.

"I heard my name. Is there a question you have about me and my ex?"

The other girls mumbled, not wanting our night to go up in flames.

"Damn, you had to be all in my business to hear me even say your fucking name."

I blinked a few times, trying to gather the pieces of ember falling off of me. Getting disrespectful with me wasn't the move.

"Mika, you know me because of Nikki. You know enough about me to know that I mind my business. When I tend to confront people minding my business, lips get busted and faces get knotted the fuck up."

Shayna sighed heavily, already sensing that I wasn't about to calm down as easily as she'd hoped.

Just to ease her mind, I said, "I'm calm." It was a complete lie, but she didn't need to know that. Mika had dug her hole months ago, and I was ready to throw the dirt on top of her.

"Speaking of Nikki, I think you wanna be with her. The way you look at her is telling." Mika snickered and sipped her drink. Her comment had everyone else at the table on mute.

"Mika—" Shayna started to speak up, but I stopped her.

"You wish you had someone to look at you like that, Mika."

Everyone gasped.

"I mean, besides the other ladies sitting at this table who are afraid to say anything to you. Thing is, you know damn well I'm not the one. I'll smack every nerve root out ya mouth without blinking."

Instead of shutting the fuck up, she found some soul inside the glass she sipped from.

"Much to my displeasure, Nikki may be your friend. But you'll *never* be anything more. So stop pining away for my girl and find you a man who makes you want him as much as you want Nikki. Thirsty bitch." She mumbled that last part.

"The only thing I'm thirsty for is a felony, battery to be specific."

"Sounds exactly like where you need to be. You ghetto ass, broke bitch. Who comes to a restaurant like this in fucking ripped up jeans? A broke bitch is who."

Her wink was as if she reached out and punched me. I had to return the favor.

"Poppi!"

Diving over the centerpiece in front of us, I caught Mika before she tried backing away from the table. In less than a second, the beautiful centerpiece I'd been admiring mere minutes ago, was destroyed by my knee digging into it. Glasses fell, drinks spilled, and table decorations shifted. I grabbed a handful of Mika's hair and yanked her across the table. Security busted into the room to try and get order.

"Poppi!"

Everyone was busy trying to pry me off of Mika, who laughed once she was free.

"Look at you! Looking a fucking mess and can't even hold yourself together in this expensive ass restaurant! Dirty, hood rat, bitch!"

I snatched out of Shayna's and Qita's hold and glared at Mika, ready to kick my heels off and stomp a bitch.

Then, I remembered... Nikki.

"You know what..." Snatching my clutch off the table, I stormed toward the exit of the dinner room with Shayna begging me to stay. If I stayed, I would surely leave this restaurant in handcuffs. At the door, Memphis's goon stopped me.

"No one in or out," his voice lowly boomed. He held a smirk, though.

"That applies to Nikki; not me." Sailing past him, I ignored him telling me to stop. Steps out of the restaurant, I glanced over my shoulder to see another one of Memphis's goons on my trail.

I shook my head, frustrated and heated. It would've taken nothing for me to walk back in there and drag Mika all the way back to Pensacola. I fled inside the first establishment I came upon just to dodge Memphis's fucking goons.

My night couldn't get any worse.

MEMPHIS

"Aye, is that Poppi?"

Everything around me ceased at the mention of her name. Eddie wasn't even talking to me, but my head whipped around to see where he'd spotted her. For sure, Poppi strutted her fine ass across the packed club to the bar.

"The fuck is she doin' here?" Nikki and her bridal party were supposed to be at the club next door. I made special arrangements for security and everything just so they could enjoy themselves. Taking my phone out of my pocket, I went to call Nikki when I saw she'd texted me. Just then, my phone rang. It was Quell, the head of my security.

"Yeah!" I barked into the phone. I couldn't hear shit.

"Poppi skipped the party."

"I see her. I see you, too."

Hanging up on him, I checked Nikki's message.

Nikki: Poppi left dinner and isn't answering my calls. Will you call her and see where the hell she is?

I thought it was cute that Nikki added Poppi's number like I didn't have that shit. Just to ease Nikki's mind, I texted her back.

Me: I got her. Enjoy ya night.

Nikki: Thank you, bro. Love you!

Me: I love you.

"Yeah, that is Poppi," Boston stated. "Let me call my wife and see what the hell is goin' on."

Standing to my feet, I said, "Nah, I got it."

As I left VIP, security followed. A nigga was already in Hood's face, causing my growl to war with the base of the speakers. Before I could step to her, she'd dismissed ol' boy just for another nigga to try and make his advance. She simply grilled him. He held his hands up in surrender, tucked his tail, and retreated.

"Hood…"

Poppi's shoulders dropped at the sound of my voice behind her. She glanced at me over her shoulder and rolled her pretty brown eyes. Those eyes were like daggers sometimes. Still, I found them to be the most beautiful brown eyes I'd ever seen.

"I came in here to ease my fuckin' mind. Not be approached by every thirsty ass nigga within arm's reach. If it ain't niggas in my damn face, it's hoes tryin' me."

While she ranted, I bit into my lip and marveled at the way her plump lips glistened under the club's lighting. I had to have a taste. Somehow, my hand found its way around her neck. She acted like she didn't know the power she wielded over anyone in her presence. Honestly, that made me want her ass even more.

"It's annoying as fuck. And—"

"Rah, rah, rah… blah, blah…" I interrupted. My hand slightly tightened. "When you gon' let me rest my lips and tongue in between ya thighs?"

Her slight gasp tweaked a part of my brain that was filled with nothing but images of her mouth open as cries spilled from it while I sucked every drop from her body.

"The thought of suckin' on you is tucked so deeply into my brain… I've forgotten about any woman I've had before you."

Briefly, her eyes dipped. "You haven't had me."

Chuckling, I brought her close until we were lips to lips. "Let's remedy that. Tonight."

A couple of beats passed before she said, "No."

Turning from me, she placed her eyes back on the bartender and requested her drink. He was too busy staring at her titties spilling through the opening of the white, button-down shirt she wore.

"Aye, bruh. Don't worry 'bout it," I told him with a deep frown on my face.

"What—"

"Come with me." Without giving her the opportunity to refuse, I took her hand and led her through the thicket of people toward VIP.

"This is uncalled for," she said once we entered my section. She waved to everyone and plopped down on one of the sofas.

I sat next to her and turned her face to mine so that she could hear me. "It's not. You know you can't be out without security."

"Memphis, please. I'm without security every day."

"People know you attached to me, though."

"Yeah, now they do. First the picture and now you snatching me up to join you in VIP."

"Hood, be for real right now. I make it very clear that we're cool like that. Don't I include you in all my shit. Then there's the fact that you and Nikki are locked in for an eternity."

"And still I've been able to work and live without security. In *Ensley Heights* no less."

Licking my lips, I studied her, wishing she'd let me kiss her pouty lips. If I thought I could've done it without her drop kicking me, I would have. Niggas feared me, yet Hood didn't give a damn about that shit.

"You think so?"

She vehemently shook her head. "Don't you dare."

"I dare."

"I'll disown you, Memphis."

"You can never disown me, love." When I talked to her, I

made sure my face was close to hers. I wanted her lips to slip up and touch mine. She cutely smacked her teeth.

"I'm not Nikki. My security isn't yours to worry about."

I chuckled. "You fuckin' crazy if you think that."

Never did I play about the people in my circle. Hood knew that. All she had to do was make a phone call, and I was there. Not that she ever made a phone call for me to handle anything for her. Hood was strong as fuck and stood on her own two feet. That was one of the things I both loved and hated about her ass.

For years, I'd tried moving her shop out of Ensley Heights. She wasn't going for that shit, though. She told me she could afford to move if she wanted to, but that she wasn't about to leave her aunt's house to be neglected by people who wouldn't take care of it like she could. That shit irked my nerve. It was cool, though. I had muthafuckas watching her even if she didn't know it.

"Stop talking to me," she said seconds later as a bottle girl poured her a drink. She took it, stood, and waltzed to the front where she overlooked the rowdy crowd.

My gaze fell to the curve of her hips and down to the shapeliness of her ass. That shit was more than a handful, and my hands were large as fuck. The slits in her jeans revealed peeks of her ass cheeks. Leaning back on the sofa, I had to adjust my dick.

For a while, she was fine, drinking and bobbing to the music. That was until a couple of strippers entered the section. Hood's nose flared as her face screwed up. She pointedly glared at me as the niggas went crazy. Liquor had them all acting like they'd never seen a naked bitch before. Meanwhile, I'd barely had two drinks and could give a fuck about any woman except Hood.

Flight was written all over her face, prompting me to warn her.

"You betta not!"

She glared harder, but I blew a kiss at her, infuriating her even more. I loved getting under her skin. Speaking of which, I stood and adjusted my dick again as I neared her. With my front to her back, she tensed with her drink stuck at her lips. My lips touched her earlobe, causing her to sharply inhale. If this shit had her about to fall apart, I knew damn well she couldn't handle my dick. That excited me as I pressed him into her ass. She gasped, and I had to snake my arm out to hold her still. The minute my hand touched the bareness of her abdomen, I knew I wasn't letting this night end without Hood being underneath me.

Slowly, I swayed, bringing her along. Once she caught my rhythm, I moved my hand down to rest on her thigh, right next to her pussy. Her hand landed on top of mine, and that was when I knew I had her. Her head tilted to the side, inviting me to taste her skin right there. I opened wide and sucked a hefty portion of her neck. As I squeezed her thigh, her hand squeezed mine. If I moved my fingers just a hair to the right, they'd be resting on her mound.

"What're we gon' do about this fire, Hood?" I whispered in her ear.

She exhaled a deep breath and pinched her eyes shut. Darkly, I chuckled in her ear.

"Memphis!"

Hood stiffened in my arms as Daphne's high-pitched tone met her ears. Before I could think, she was out of my arms. I grabbed her arm to keep her from going far. Eyes blazing, I grilled Daphne who stood outside of the section with her homegirls looking just as dumb as she thought she looked.

"Aye!" I barked to security. "Get them the fuck outta here!"

Daphne didn't like that shit. She threw her clutch at me,

hitting me upside my head. I didn't give a fuck about the hurt written all over her face. If she couldn't take a clue that a nigga was really done with her, then she'd keep getting her feelings hurt. I hated the fucking attention she brought to us and more importantly how this shit just fucked up the mood between me and Hood. Then there was the blaring question of how the fuck Daphne found me. Her invitation to Nikki's bachelorette party and wedding were revoked the minute I broke things off with her.

"Watch where you throwin' shit, bitch!"

I had to hold tight to Hood. She wanted to jump the banister separating the section from the walk thru just so she could jump on Daphne. People had their phones out, waiting for anything to get worse than it was.

"Chill, my baby," I told Hood who wasn't trying to hear that shit.

"Fuck you, bitch! That's my nigga!" Daphne hollered while security hauled her ass away.

"Come get yo' nigga then, hoe!"

I looked at Hood like she was crazy.

"The fuck." I grilled her ass and got into her face, my anger now mirroring hers. "Watch what the fuck comin' outcha mouth," I blasted. "We both know who the fuck I belong to." That was the first time I shut Hood up so quickly. She retreated back to the sofa and sat down.

Swiping my hand over my face, I scanned the section, and everything was back to normal as if nothing happened. Boston stood at the entrance with his hands in his pockets, observant. Eddie sat on the other sofa pretending like he wasn't enjoying one of the strippers in front of him throwing her ass in a circle. He was scared to do any fucking thing around me, and I loved

THE HOOD FLOWER GIRL

that. The rest of the niggas surrounded the other stripper, throwing money at her. In my head, I wondered which one of these niggas dropped my fucking location. Boston was the only nigga I trusted with my life. The rest of these niggas were Eddie's family and friends.

Moving to Boston's side, I slipped my hands into my pockets as well and looked out over the crowd.

"The more we try to step away from the street shit, the more we gotta show niggas the streets ain't never left us."

Agreeing, I dapped Boston. If a nigga was quick to give a bitch my location, he could just as easily drop that shit to the opps. As soon as I found out who the snake was, his ass was as good as skinned.

CHAPTER 5

POPPI

After Daphne's duck ass popped up, my night swiftly went to the deepest parts of hell. Memphis wouldn't let me move an inch, and he even stopped me from having a third drink. Not only was I angry, but I couldn't even get lit on the count of him. Two hours of that shit, and I was ready to walk my ass back to the suite.

"You'll leave when I do."

Memphis really thought he could order me around just because I gave in to him once or twice. That was the problem with niggas in power. You gave them an inch and the next thing you know, they've got you tied to a damn bed. The thought had me squirming in my seat and clamping my legs together.

"You good?"

I plastered a mug on my face and didn't bother looking at Memphis. Instead, I prayed the ride back to the hotel would've been quicker than the thirty minutes it was supposed to take.

Memphis's hand grabbed my thigh and squeezed. "You hear me talkin' to you, shawty?"

No, I didn't hear him. Because, at his touch, blood rushed through my ears. Recalling how he lowkey danced with me, I had to bite my lip to keep from groaning. Memphis had a dick on him that left its searing imprint on my ass. His chuckle brought me back to the backseat of the sedan carrying us back to our hotel.

He claimed that he belonged to me, rendering me speechless. The rest of the night, I'd watched Memphis too closely. I observed the way he interacted with Boston, and the way he didn't interact with anyone else. Then there was the way he curved any woman who attempted to talk to him, wave, or anything. I felt like he was doing that shit just because he knew I was there and didn't want to fuck up his chances of us ending the night with each other. Truthfully…he had me as good as wrapped around his dick before Daphne showed up.

My thoughts were interrupted by a message from Nikki. She and Shayna had been blowing my phone up. Of course, I ignored them. Nikki needed to enjoy her night and not worry about me. This was why I didn't want to come to Atlanta in the first damn place.

Nikki: I love you, sis.

I put my phone on do not disturb and dropped it inside my clutch.

"If you heard that phone, you heard me talkin' to you," Memphis said. His hand was gone from my thigh, but the heat stayed. His phone rang seconds later.

"Nikki, baby, I told you everything's good."

His phone was on speaker. From the sound of it, Nikki's

dinner party was still in full swing. I smiled, grateful that my slight interruption didn't totally fuck up her night.

"I need to talk to Poppi to believe it," Nikki countered.

"You don't trust me?" Memphis was such a businessman. I rolled my eyes the second I heard Nikki's heavy sigh. Just that quickly, she folded.

"Okay, okay. Will you at least tell her that I love her?"

This time it was my turn to sigh. I hated having issues with Nikki's other friends and cousins, but none of them fucked with me either. Just because I didn't like them didn't mean I had to make Nikki choose between us, which was why I offered to be the flower girl. Nikki had known Shayna and Mika longer than me. Although our bond was deep, I loved her enough to take pressure off her in times like this.

"I got you, baby. Now get back to ya party."

Nikki mumbled, "Okay," and hung up the phone.

"You got my lil' baby stressed." Memphis chuckled as the chauffeur finally maneuvered into the hotel's parking lot.

He pulled up to the front, and I waited for Memphis to come open my door. Once I stood on the street beside him, he reached for my hand. Because my feet were a little sore in these heels, I banded my hand around two of his fingers. They were so thick and long that they were still visible when I looked down to mentally log the joining of our hands. Ironically, the fingers I held were tattooed with nothing other than a plethora of tiny flowers. Those flowers grew to larger ones the further up his wrist and arm they went.

"One day when you stop fuckin' runnin' from me, I'll show you what's hidin' in them."

He caught me staring, and I wasn't even aware that we were on the elevator. I let my hand release his fingers and cleared my throat, suddenly hot. As soon as the elevator opened on the tenth floor, I was off of it, hauling ass to my suite. In front of my door, I stopped to glance back at Memphis. He stood at his door with his hands stuffed in his pockets. I wanted him to bite down on my nipples the way his glistening teeth bit down on his bottom lip.

Rushing inside my suite, I closed the door behind me and plastered myself against it just so I could catch my breath. Groaning, I stripped and went inside the bathroom to shower. As water washed over my head and body, I recalled how Memphis's body being so close to mine felt. He was so much taller and bigger than me. Against him, I just felt…sheltered and *loved*.

My stomach growled, reminding me that I hadn't eaten. Dashing away thoughts of Memphis, I thoroughly washed and rinsed my body, then stepped from the steamy shower feeling drained. Hopefully, once I got some food inside me, this feeling would flee. Moisturized and dressed, I decided to order myself some room service. I sat on the sofa watching television until a knock sounded at the door. Barefoot, I padded to the door in a hurry because my stomach was growling worse now than before.

On the other side of the door, Memphis's grill met me. His ass was in nothing but some gray sweatpants, black socks, and black designer slides. All the ice he had on earlier was gone, except the grill. Immaculate was the only word I could use to describe the ink covering his hard chest. He held my food in one hand and a bottle of wine in the other.

"Come on," he said. "Lemme feed you."

Memphis was high as fuck. His voice was deep, exotic, and caused my clit to jump in anticipation as if she knew he was going to be sucking on her soon. My eyes traveled the length of his body and focused in on the bow of his legs. There were certain things about Memphis that I refused to acknowledge. Like the way his powerful legs could hold me up against any one of these walls.

"Come with me, baby…"

Breathless, my eyes flew to his. With only my phone and clutch in hand, I closed the door behind myself and followed Memphis to his suite. Before he even opened the door, the strong presence of marijuana wafted into my nose. Walking inside of his suite felt like I was leading myself to certain heartbreak. Still, when he discarded his slides at the door and turned to walk backward as his eyes sailed down my half-naked body, I was ready for whatever. The interior looked no different than my suite, except his was dimly lit, with the television tuned in to Pandora. I liked that he was playing R&B.

"Strip," he softly demanded.

Gulping, I placed my phone and clutch by his slides and removed my blue, silk pajama shorts, then let the button-down matching top join the material on the floor. Memphis must've licked his thick lips a hundred times. He sat the covered dish on the coffee table followed by the wine. As his body shifted, I couldn't help but notice the protrusion of the object between his thighs.

"Come get it."

Every statement that dripped from his lips sounded like he was about to fuck me up. Yet my feet carried me right to him. Our lips were like two ships colliding. Neither of us could wait for this moment, and now that it was here, we had no patience for shit resembling anything soft.

Memphis's herbal tongue entered my mouth as my arms surrounded his strong neck. His hands cupped my ass so hard, I gasped into his mouth. All he wanted to do was pull me closer as he kissed me, so that I could feel how hard his dick was. He bit his way over my jawline and down my neck while I reached into his sweats to wrap my hand around the girth of his long dick.

"Fuck..." he mumbled in between bites. His head lowered to my nipples as my fingers trailed the length of him until I reached his tip. It was already wet there. Like I hoped he'd bite my stiff nipples, he did. From pleasure, I whimpered.

Since there was no turning back now, I dropped to my knees and pulled his sweats all the way to his ankles. He grabbed a fistful of my hair as he stepped out of the sweats. The look on his face was savagely sexy. Especially when his teeth sank into that wet bottom lip.

"Don't get up 'til that muhfucka is empty," he dictated.

With my eyes boldly stapled to his, I took both hands and wrapped them around him. I spit on his tip, then slowly swiveled my saliva around his fat head. His grip on my roots tightened, yet I hadn't even started showing him just how quickly I could make him bow out. Then, while he recovered, I could actually eat my food.

Removing one of my hands, I made way for my mouth to envelop him. His thighs tensed, and he groaned deep in his throat. My clit throbbed as I closed my eyes and let my mouth and tongue follow along to Tank's crooning.

"Oooh, fuck..."

The deeper I took him inside my wet mouth, the more he moaned. Saliva coated the hand massaging his straining length. Feeling like I'd tortured him enough, I took him down my throat and enjoyed the sound he made. Expertly, I bobbed on his dick, then used my other hand to handle the heaviness of his balls. Because I was greedy like that, I slipped his dick from my mouth and used my tongue to take each one of them into my mouth. I never missed paying attention to his dick, massaging him from root to tip.

"Shit!" he belted.

Only then did I allow myself the pleasure of watching him release. For he was right there. As soon as popped his beautiful, dark chocolate, thick length back into my mouth, it was over for him. Listening to him cum was my new favorite music. Nothing beat the sound of him growling my name while I swallowed every silky drop of his tasteful essence.

MEMPHIS

Going to the cemetery was the most difficult part of losing my grandmother, but I had to come share this accomplishment with her before anyone else. As I neared the spot where her plot lay, a familiar frame was there, on her knees replacing old flowers with new ones.

Placing my car in park, I got out, surprised to see Hood here. Her back was to me as I approached her. My shadow fell over her, causing her to glance over her shoulder. The sight of me lit her face up. Shyly, she spoke.

"Everything okay?" she asked when I didn't immediately respond back.

How could a nigga like me explain to Hood that she was the first girl I ever met who rendered me speechless. On the streets I was sure, almost cocky. The same went for the classroom. I was always sure about my fucking moves. With Hood, I wasn't sure about shit. Except the fact that she made a nigga want her.

"Yeah," I replied.

"What's that in your hand?"

Hell, I glanced down at the folded-up paper, forgetting for a second why I was even here.

"I'm graduating in a few weeks," I told her. Four years of college had been a breeze for me. Almost to the point where I was contemplating on going for my masters.

She beamed up at me, that blinding ass smile was spectacular under the high-set sun.

"Congratulations, Memphis! I'm proud of you!"

It was as if those words were spoken by both Hood and my grandmother. That shit hit my damn soul.

Long before that time, I'd fallen in love with Hood. When I went away to school, she was always on my mind. Every time I slid back into town, I made it a point to see her. Over the years, I'd met plenty of women who fit the role of "the one". However, they weren't Hood. Hood had a special place in my heart where no one else existed. Not even my grandmother. This place was reserved for the woman I would love forever. It was reserved for the woman I would give my children to, and the woman I wanted to make a future with. Hood owned that spot in me. She solidified her place the day she beat the brakes off that girl who was bullying Nikki. I had so much respect for Hood, and her ability to be both soft and strong.

So, when I yanked her up off the floor and carried her to the bedroom, I had no problems showing her just how much I cared about her. It wasn't shit for me to bounce back. This dick had her name written on it and would brick up whenever she fucking *thought* about the shit. None too gently, I placed her in the middle of the bed and followed her there. I buried my head in her neck and kissed her there before trailing them down. She was hot all over, arching her back and with her hands she begged me to move lower.

"I got you, baby," I assured her. Hood's body was soft as fuck and curved like she was sculpted with the sharpest, yet most delicate knife. Her taut nipples were too tight for me to ignore them. I sucked them one at a time, even as my nose flared from the scent of her pussy dripping.

Reaching between her thighs, I slid my fingers between her wet, plump lips and groaned my pleasure at how close she was to falling apart. Her faces were beautiful, each one I mentally logged to replay later. On her next cry, I plunged two fingers deep into her, damn near nutting at how quickly she came.

"Memphis!" she brokenly cried. Her thighs were wide open

and shook like fuck. Staring at her pussy eat my fingers had to be the second-best thing I loved to watch her body do.

"This fat ass pussy is so tight. You got my fingers sloppy, too." I loved how she spread her legs wider and propped her feet on my shoulders. She wanted me to see everything her pussy was doing.

"I love the way you sucked my dick, Hood." As I moved lower, I didn't give a fuck that she was in the throes of another orgasm. I took her clit into my mouth, plunged my fingers even deeper, and sent her ass further into space. Her fingernails dug into my Caeser cut as she repeatedly gasped. The more her pussy squirted the more I fucking drank. My tongue lashed her like I was punishing her, and the reward was endless amounts of cum spilling from her tight ass pussy.

Feeling how heavy my dick was, I knew he was ready too. Slipping my fingers from her middle, I pushed her thighs all the way back to clean up the mess we made. By the time I positioned my dick at the entrance my fingers had just left, Hood was a teary-eyed mess. Her eyes were dazed, and she repeatedly mumbled something that I couldn't make out.

The second my head mated with her pussy's juices, this nigga knew he was where the fuck he was supposed to be. As I pushed inside her soft, warm, wet walls, we both lost our shit. Loudly, she gasped at the intrusion. I whimpered like a bitch and didn't give one fuck. This pussy was mine.

I stretched her open, hoarsely grunting every time my balls smacked her ass. She moved her hips perfectly, the sensation prickling a nigga's skin. Our eyes locking to the clap of our bodies had to be something more binding than the bond our souls already had.

"I knew this dick was yours, Hood," I taunted. "He wanna bust so deep inside you."

"Oooh!" she moaned long and loud as her body erupted.

Growling and pumping furiously into her, I let her pussy suck every drop of my cum out of me just like her fucking throat had. I held my body above hers, breathing hardly as we continued to stare into each other's eyes. With my dick still resting inside her, I leaned down to bring our tongues together. The lock they made was as good a sign as any that neither one of us were going anywhere.

Sometime later, after I'd cleaned us both, Hood lay across the bed knocked out. I slipped from the room to heat her food up and grab us a water. Within minutes, I was back in the bedroom. Placing the plate and waters on the bed, I leaned close to her ear and kissed her.

"Wake up and eat, baby."

Slowly she came to. We ended the night with her naked body straddling my lap while I fed her.

CHAPTER 6

POPPI

Over in the night, my phone kept going off. Grumbling, I left the warmth of Memphis's arms banded around me to reach for my phone.

Shayna: Girl, where are you! I keep calling!
Me: I'm safe and fine. I'll see you at brunch.

Placing the phone back on the nightstand, I was back pinned between Memphis's arms in seconds. They were heavy, corded, and smelled fresh from the shower we'd had. My hand rested on his hard back, not caring that this was too intimate and way too personal for something that would never happen again. His chin rested on my forehead as he lightly breathed. Unexpectedly, his hand moved to my thigh and hiked it back over his like it was before I moved. His thigh rested between my thighs, cradled right against my sex. Then he moved his hand to lay on the swell of my ass.

"You belong next to me, every fuckin' night, Hood."

The rumble of his deep voice vibrated against every nerve in my body and swallowed my heart whole. I wouldn't mumble a word, not even to agree. Because even if that was how I felt, it didn't matter. Feelings and reality were two different things. I could've very well followed my feelings and ended up broken for the rest of my life. Or I could've stuck to reality and pretended like I hadn't been in love with this man since the moment I knew his name. Minutes later, I dozed off to the sound of him lightly snoring.

Something heavy positioned itself between my legs. Slowly, I cracked my eyes open to see Memphis staring down at me.

"I gotta get you to brunch on time," he said, then softly kissed my lips. A smirk covered the lips he'd kissed so much last night that they were still tender and swollen. Some part of me should've felt ashamed for the shit I did last night, but I was too ready to experience just a touch of him again. Just this one last time.

"What if I'm not ready to leave?" I breathlessly questioned. His answer was to part my thighs even more and position them in the crooks of his arms. His dick was hard and rested against my sore sex.

"Put me in," he ordered. Needing no further commands, I took his heavy dick into my hands and guided him to my center. She was ready; just the thought of him being back inside of her enough to cause an earthquake inside there.

As he entered me, his face fell into the crook of my neck. I palmed the back of his head and let my nails graze his shoulders. The deeper he sank, my pink toes curled, and my mouth drooped open.

Last night was rough and raw. Right now, Memphis slowly

rocked back and forth inside me. Yet this onslaught was just as effective as if he were ramming inside me. My pussy loved it and rewarded him within a few short seconds.

"I just wanna show you that I can make love to you too," he said. "I can beat it up, or I can slow it down and make you fall in love with me."

I shrieked loudly, convulsing like I was in a bed of livewires. He held my hips off the bed and slowly worked me until I was building toward an even stronger orgasm.

"You gon' fall in love with me, Hood? Hm?"

Closing my eyes against the intensity in his, I focused on giving him something else to think about. I moved my hips to meet his and relished in him groaning. The question was forgotten as he dropped his head and watched his dick slide slowly in and out of me. That was all it took to release the dam holding back the juice he sought.

Grunting, he picked up his pace and kept his eyes glued to the mess I was making all over his dick. One thing was for sure: if I wasn't in love with Memphis before he bedded me, I was damn sure up a fucking creek now. Giving him and his dick up was getting more complicated with each thrust and with each touch of his lips to mine.

An hour later when I emerged from the bathroom showered, teeth and face refreshed, Memphis had an outfit and shoes laid out on the bed for me. It had slipped my mind that my things were back in my suite.

"Where'd you get this stuff from?" All of it was designer, and the slides were nicer than any pair I owned. I picked them up first, observing the beading along the front part.

"The boutique downstairs," he replied. "They have some nice shit in there."

The white linen short set he picked out fit my taste to a T. So did the slides. This man even had the forethought to purchase me a clutch to match the new outfit.

"Aren't you sweet," I quipped. He walked up to me shirtless and wearing a pair of black boxers. I should've known by now just how good this man looked naked. Still, I was taken aback by his sexiness. He dropped a quick kiss on my lips.

"That ain't nothin'. Now get dressed before Nikki starts blowin' my phone up."

Chuckling, I disrobed and moisturized myself before donning my clothes. He watched me the whole time, barely getting himself dressed while watching the show. Nikki, the girls, and I would start our day off with brunch, then find a few stores to shop in. I wasn't particularly down with that last part. I was not willing to break my bank on things I would barely wear. I'd put a smile on my face and bear it, though. Especially after last night.

Once Memphis informed me that our ride was ready, I slid into my slides and swiped the new clutch off the bed. I grabbed my old clutch from the foyer's floor, so that I could transfer my things to the new one. On the ride down to the lobby, I relished in Memphis's hold on my hand. This was the type of stuff I'd miss. That and the way his dick and tongue just knew how to work me.

Inside the car, I started removing things from my clutch to put it inside the new one. Upon opening the new clutch, a wad of money and a black card were tucked in there. None of which were mine.

"Uhm... Memphis. Whose clutch is this?"

He leaned over and seized my mouth.

"Yours, baby. I want you to enjoy your day. Since we're together now, it's time to come to some compromises."

I leaned back from his kiss to mug him.

"Together?"

"*Together*. What you'on wanna be with me?"

Chuckling, I sat back in the seat and waved Memphis off. "You must be crazy."

"Nah, *you* crazy, my baby." He went to looking cool and calm, to savage in a heartbeat. "I was up in you without a care in the fuckin' world. I gave you too many of my fuckin' kids. Matter fact, you as good as pregnant. What we gon' name our first child? Memphis?" He smoothed his hand over his beard. "Yeah, that can work for my son or daughter."

I busted out laughing at the look on his face. This nigga was sitting here actually staring off into space like he could see the future where his children were actually present.

"Our kids gon' be spoiled as fuck. Can you imagine having a smart, fine ass mama and a rich as fuck daddy. Shiiidd."

"Wait." I snickered. "First of all, *we're not together*." I slowed it down just so he could understand what the hell I said.

"Aight," he concurred too easily. His chuckle that followed didn't sound so cute as he tweaked my chin.

"And second of all, I'm on birth control."

"Fuck a damn pill. Stop takin' that shit."

An icy trail of uneasiness slid through me from the way he stared at me with that damn snarl on his face. He stared until we were sitting in front of the restaurant where brunch was to take place. With eyebrows drawn together, I watched him get out of the sedan to come around and open my door.

Without thinking, I took his proffered hand and joined him on the sidewalk. His large hands cupped my face to bring me to him for a deep kiss. I held onto his arms and angled my head so that he could get as much as he wanted.

He broke the kiss and grinned down at me. "And you think you don't belong to me." There was that chuckle again. "Yeah, aight."

"Memphis..."

He shushed me and kissed my lips again. "You look sexy as fuck. Gon' on in there and enjoy ya food." The mug on his face contradicted everything he said.

"Why are you looking like that?"

"'Cause I wanna take you back to the hotel and fuck on you some mo'."

Smacking my teeth, I shook my head. He took that as his cue to kiss all over my cheek.

"Gon' 'fore I change my mind."

Rolling my eyes, I let him open the door for me, then waited for the server to direct me to the rest of the party. No matter how much I wanted to forgo this shit, nothing was going to get me out of the state of bliss that I was in. The girls sat at a long table to the right, each of their faces reflecting shock.

"What?" I asked as I sat next to Nikki. She, too, wore a shocked expression. I placed my clutch on the table regarding them like they were crazy. Mika's expression was especially stank. At the very end of the table, she practically seethed.

"Memphis was just all over you," Nikki finally said. My face burned, realizing they'd seen the entire interaction between me and Memphis.

A second later, I reminded her, "I thought that was what you wanted."

Nikki's eyes rounded before she shrieked with joy. Then, she had the nerve to tear up.

"Aww, this is so perfect, Poppi!"

The only other person who felt Nikki's sentiments was

Shayna. She jumped out of her seat and came over to hug me from the back.

"'Bout time!" she added.

"Y'all are actin' like that nigga just proposed to me," I said to Shayna's back. I wasn't even Memphis's girl. We spent one night and morning together. That did not equate to a relationship.

He just said that the two of you are together.

"The biggest hurdle has been scaled. Now—"

"Now nothing," I interjected. Bummed, Nikki started to whine.

"May I get you a drink, ma'am?"

I was grateful for the server reappearing. Once he brought me my mimosa, I could hopefully get some of these nerves out of me. My body was still on fire from Memphis fucking the life out of it.

"Poppi—"

"Drop it, Nikki," I mumbled.

Reluctantly, she did so. Whatever they were talking about before I joined them picked right back up. I tuned out a minute later when my phone chirped. Removing it from my clutch, I nearly smiled at Memphis's name flashing across my screen. I held it together, though. Every pair of eyes sitting at the table trained on me.

Memphis: We ARE together. Just thought I'd remind you. And stop takin' those fuckin' pills. I'm serious as fuck.

Me: NO, we're NOT… You'll forget all about me once this weekend is over.

Seconds later, Memphis called my phone.

"Hello," I answered nonchalantly.

"Look out the window."

My eyes bounced up off the table to focus out of the window.

Memphis stood on the curb, propped up against the sedan we just exited, with one of his hands in his pocket.

"You need me to come in there and—"

"No, no..." I hurried and said. "I'll talk to you later."

Even after I hung up, Memphis stood outside for a minute undoubtedly warring with himself as to whether or not he should crash this brunch. His ass was definitely good for some shit like that. My body shivered at the monster I'd undoubtedly created.

THE HOOD FLOWER GIRL

MEMPHIS

"Next Tuesday at 2 is good."

My face balled up at the possibility that Boston was putting more shit on my plate. At the dining table, I sat across from him and mugged him. As soon as he hung up, I was on his ass.

"I thought we weren't discussing business while on this trip. And we're booked as fuck next week." I was already trying to figure out how to move some shit around so that I could see Hood every day next week. She thought I was bullshitting, but her little ass wasn't going anywhere. Hell, I already had our wedding colors picked out.

Boston chuckled and then mugged me back. "That ain't business, nigga. I gotta start counseling."

My face went from being balled up, to being concerned. Boston was my nigga, and we talked to each other about everything. If something was wrong with him, something was wrong with me. That was just the way me and this nigga moved.

"You good, bruh?"

"Yeah, I'm cool, mane." Exasperation laced his sigh, then he shrugged. "Tryna save my damn marriage."

"Damn, for real? I mean, yeah, y'all got normal couple issues, but nothing that should warrant y'all walkin' away from each other. It's barely been a year." Here I was, a nigga who had never been married, trying to hand out advice.

"That's the thing. Neither of us are tryna walk away. Things just been crazy as fuck. My schedule, being away from home all the time...all that shit is just piling the fuck up."

We did travel a lot, especially over these last few months. McCorvey & Kelly was a force to be reckoned with and that was because we stayed on the grind.

"When this deal with the Tornadoes is done, we gon' take a much-needed break." Trying to acquire a football team was taxing. The current owners were giving us hell, but I wasn't backing out of the deal for anything.

"To be honest, it's not even this deal. It's just been…crazy," he finished. Just then Eddie walked up to the table, looking aggravated.

"What's the problem?" Boston asked, effectively cutting off the subject of him and his wife. His business wasn't shared with anyone outside of us. Since Eddie was marrying Nikki, Boston and I promised Nikki to start including him more. So far, I ain't had to chop the nigga down.

"This wedding shit is stressing me the fuck out," he admitted.

Two pairs of eyes cocked at him. The rest of the party hadn't trickled in yet, probably still fucked up from last night. Honestly, those niggas could've stayed where the fuck they were at just in case Boston and I had to catch a body.

"The fuck you mean?" Boston and I barked at the same time.

Eddie threw his hands up and sputtered. "Damn, y'all chill out. I thought I could speak my peace without y'all jumpin' down my fuckin' throat. Who the fuck else would y'all rather I talk to?"

Now I was shifting in my seat. This nigga was about to piss me the fuck off. My heat was locked and loaded, ready to light him up if he said some sideways shit.

"A preacha, nigga," Boston said.

Eddie busted out laughing. "Damn, y'all act like I said I'on wanna marry Nikki or somethin'. Which ain't even close to the fuckin' case. *This wedding shit* is stressing me the fuck out. That's what the fuck I said."

"So what? You wanna go to the courthouse like I did?" Boston questioned.

Eddie threw his hands up. "Hell, yeah. I preferred that shit. Nikki wanted all this extra shit. Look, the other niggas ain't even here yet. Got us sittin' here waiting on them. Mind you, all this shit is for show."

Boston and I both sat quietly reflecting on how we wanted to proceed. Again, I wasn't the nigga to offer advice. When it came to weddings, I wasn't well-versed in that shit either. I was Boston's best man and, admittedly, I couldn't vibe with the whole courthouse situation either. But if my homeboy liked it, I loved it for him.

"Have you told Nikki? Being honest with her is where you should've first fuckin' started." He could sit here and cry to us, but his loyalty and openness should've been with Nikki first.

"Nah, I haven't talked to her. I'm not tryna ruin this for her."

"Then don't," Boston simply stated. "This shit is what you make it. You don't give her this, she'll never forgive you. Besides, this shit is petty, my nigga. Give my girl her wedding before you fuck it up."

"And do that shit with a fuckin' smile on yo' face," I added.

Again, Eddie cracked up.

"Don't make me have to knock all them teeth outcha face," I threatened.

Boston chuckled as he stared at the still laughing Eddie. "That shit funny ain't it?" he drawled.

"Y'all niggas need to chill," Eddie finally mumbled.

Like Boston, I eyed Eddie, searching for the smallest piece of thread I could pull to see if this nigga was on some bullshit. Because if he was, it wasn't going to be any wedding. It was most definitely going to be a celebration of life, though.

Three hours later, I didn't give a fuck about nothing as I called Hood's phone for the second time. I gave her the benefit of the doubt for missing my first call. Missing my second call was about to have me pulling up to her location, which was some fucking spa not far from my location. My face contorted while wondering if she was laying up in that bitch butt ass naked.

I called again.

"Hello?" she answered breathlessly.

"Aye," I drawled. "Is you naked?"

"What?"

"What the fuck you got on, baby?"

"Clothes, Memphis. What are you talking about?"

"Why you ain't answer my call?"

"Is there a reason for this call?"

"You'on miss me? That's fucked up, Hood."

She snickered, and I imagined that her cheeks darkened.

"Don't you have something else to be doing? Like watching a game?" I can barely hear you, so I know you can't hear me."

"I hear you loud and clear, baby. The game is almost over, so I'm tryna catch up with you. Ditch ya girls and come spend some time with me."

"Now you know that's not possible. And last night was just last night—"

"Don't make me pull up, Hood."

She audibly smacked her teeth. "You're really serious, huh?"

"I am. Why the fuck would I play about anything that has to do with us?"

She was quiet for a few beats, then heavily sighed. "I'm not ditching my girls. You'll have to wait to see me when it's convenient for me."

The silence in my ear had me heated like a muthafucka. I let her live, though. This streetball game was lit, but I was ready to go. My fingers were itching to either work or get my hands on Hood. Downtime was at a minimum with me. I was a wealthy nigga because of the grind and hustle in me.

If my grandmother was still alive, I know she'd be proud of me. After graduating college, Boston and I came off the streets and put our education to use. We weren't particularly *clean*, but we kept shit clean. Either way it went, we were making money and proving that the street life wasn't the only way to a multi-million-dollar life. To think, all I wanted to do was make my grandmother happy. Now I was living life, seeing more money than even she or my parents had ever touched.

Speaking of my parents, I glanced at the text from my pops, wanting to straight up ignore that shit.

Pops: Have you talked to ya mama?

Seeing that shit had me heated as fuck. If my mama was ignoring him, his ass must've fucked up again. Shaking my head, I dialed my mama's number to see if she would answer.

"Hello, baby boy," she answered on the first ring. "Oh, it's loud in the background."

"Hey, Ma. You aight?"

"Of course, I am," she replied, a little too cheerily.

"Pops is lookin' for you." Being the referee for him was bullshit. His ass was too fucking grown to be out here *still* fucking around on my mama.

"He'll find out where I'm at in a few days," she replied, nonplussed. "Since you all in my business, I'm at Nore's office filing for the divorce I should've asked for twenty years ago."

Although I wasn't surprised, my heart dropped. Like Nikki, there was still a small amount of hope I harbored for my parents, but I couldn't be mad at my mama.

"'Bout time, Ma. Find you a house, and I got you."

She chortled. "Son, I am already five steps ahead of you. Remember the house my parents owned? I never got rid of it. All my things will be moved in by the time I get back. What you can do for me is not repeat the same shit your father did. I don't have to explain because you already know."

I did…too well.

"I thought I was doing what was best for you and Nikki by staying with him. Thankfully, my stupidity didn't rub off on my daughter, and I'm praying his philandering ways didn't rub off on you. Sleeping around is one thing when you're single. But as a married man…you should never."

"I know, Ma." I wanted to hop on the highway and find my pops just so that I could beat his ass for breaking my mama's heart. She would never forgive me, though. As much as she hated Jonathan's ways, she loved him. Plus, she wholeheartedly believed in respecting your elders. I didn't want my life cut short just because I couldn't control my anger when it came to the man who took part in giving me life. He had his duty to uphold, and he fucked it up. My only obligation was upholding my duty and that was to respect my mother and father. Jonathan would be dealt with by someone more powerful and superior than me. I was cool with that.

"I love you, Son."

"I love you too. I'll be back in the city in a few days. You gon' be aight 'til then."

She chuckled. "I'ma be on a plane as soon as I walk out of here."

I laughed with my mama. "I'm proud of you. Don't let me have to put a bullet in a nigga, though. Bring somebody home who's gon' make Pops lose his fuckin' mind."

"Memphis!" She scoffed, then busted out into more laughter. She knew I was right.

Even though I was proud of my mama, as I hung up, I couldn't help but feel like shit. My pops was the first nigga to break the cycle in my family. Every McCorvey man who came before him married and remained faithful. Then again, every nigga had it in him to remain faithful. Some niggas were just more selfish than a muthafucka and no matter what a woman did to and for them, they were destined to be no good. That's the group of niggas Jonathan fucking McCorvey was lumped into.

CHAPTER 7

POPPI

Heartbreak wasn't something to tussle with. I was really good with my hands…my heart, though. There was no type of guard up when it came to Memphis. Where I thought I was strong enough to lay with him and move on, my ass was so weak that I made up some shit just to ditch these damn girls.

After Shayna left the suite, I flipped the covers back and jumped from the bed. I was half-naked as I traipsed my ass down to Memphis's room. I'd barely knocked before he answered. He reached for me and pulled me into his suite, then shut the door.

"You okay? What's wrong?" I asked him in between his kisses. He carried me to the sofa where he sat down with me in his lap. The lines in his forehead had me concerned. His fingers reached up to tuck my hair behind my ear.

"My mama filed for divorce today." He took a deep, heavy breath, then reached for the small glass on the end table. After taking a long swig of the brown liquor, he leaned his head back on the sofa and stared at the ceiling.

"I'm sorry, Memphis." My heart truly broke for him and the way his smile didn't so much as fully tip. I knew how much family meant to him. More importantly, I peeped how Memphis's relationship with his dad was always strained. Nikki never seemed to have a problem, though, so I didn't think things were terribly horrible.

"How about I order us some dinner, and we can talk if you want to."

Memphis's fingers pinched my chin. "Aight, cool."

I moved from his lap to retrace my steps to the foyer where my clutch laid on the floor. After placing our order via the hotel's app, I went into the bedroom to retrieve a blanket. Within minutes, I was back nestled in his lap with my head resting on his shoulder. He was silent, so I was too, just running my fingers over his scruffy beard while he sipped his drink. Quietly, we listened to the last inning of the baseball game he'd been watching. Now I didn't feel so bad that I skipped on going out with Nikki and the girls.

About thirty minutes later, dinner arrived. We sat on the floor and ate at the coffee table. His prayer over the food even sounded solemn. Still, as we started eating, I waited for him to open the door. If he wanted to talk, I would listen without interrupting him.

"I shouldn't be happy about it," he mumbled around a piece of steak. "But I am. My mama deserves happiness, and she doesn't have that with my pops. It's like that nigga got married and said, 'fuck you' to his wife and kids." His chuckle stemmed from a place of sadness.

"I wonder what makes a man just turn on his people. The

very people he should be the closest with are the ones he's willing to lose for fuckin' nothin'. I'll never understand. I'm twenty-eight years old and can remember the first time I realized my pops was cheating on my mama. I was in the fourth grade. He was fuckin' my teacher. Imagine going the whole school year sitting in class with the lady fuckin' ya pops. You can imagine how she must've talked about my mama." He shook his head as if he didn't want to recall those times. I surely wouldn't want to recall anything like that.

I knew as much about my father as I did about the mailman which was next to nothing. My mother raised me and Tandy until she was no longer capable. The last time I talked to her, I was in the ninth grade. I couldn't say that I missed her. She was never a huge part of me and Tandy's life. Most times, she left us with our auntie. As for Auntie Rose, she had a few boyfriends, but none that ever made her a wife. It was sad, truly, but the last boyfriend was with her for years before she passed away. And the way whoever he was would go out of his way to secretly court my auntie was pitiful. It was like she spent her life taking care of me and Tandy and working. She never got to experience the things any woman would want to…like true love.

"If I'm honest, I wanted my pops dead…more than once. But I grew up with a grandma who loved the fuck outta her son even though he was a piece of shit. As much heartache as that nigga caused my grandma, killing him would've destroyed her."

I gulped down my food, not sure why he would reveal such devious thoughts to me. Then again, some part of me felt special that he thought I was worthy of his innermost darkest thoughts.

"I respect how much you loved your grandma."

He cracked a small smile. "She was the reason for a lot of my family's success. Teaching wasn't all she did. She kept my grandfather grounded and taught him how to invest. That's aside from her teaching her grandkids how to succeed in academics."

"Which is how you graduated top ten in your class."

He made a face that caused me to cackle.

"Then you went off to college and continued to excel. That's admirable, Memphis."

After a minute, he said, "That's what she would've wanted."

If it wasn't for Mrs. McCorvey, I wouldn't have been able to see my dream of going to college. Graduating high school early provided me with enough scholarship money to complete four years of schooling. I graduated with a 4.0 grade point average and didn't once use it to step into anything corporate. Flowers were my thing. Flo's Petals was thriving, and I couldn't have asked for a better life.

"I want for my mama what my grandma had, and I think that's why it makes me so fuckin' angry. My mama deserves love."

Quietly, I assessed him. His face had relaxed some, and he was nearly done eating.

"I'm surprised to hear a man like you mention that word." Although he'd brought it up while he was buried deep in my guts. Mouth suddenly dry, I reached for my wine.

"What? Love?"

I nodded. He snorted.

"Contrary to what society has our people thinking, love is out there. Shiidd, I've been in love for a fuckin' long ass time."

Immediate and swift jealousy sliced through me. Whoever had Memphis's heart had him sitting next to me at the coffee table smiling through his anger and grief. To help swallow the clog in my throat, I nearly downed the rest of my drink.

"So how does it feel?"

I placed my nearly empty flute down and shot back, "How does what feel?" *How does it feel to know that you're in love with another woman,* I wanted to ask. *Horrid! Repulsive! I wanna stab her in the—*

"To know that I'm in love witchu?"

If anything would've been in my mouth, I surely would've choked on it. Memphis closed the space between us and kissed the dumbfounded expression off my face.

"That's a lie," I stated, while on the inside hoping that it wasn't.

"You've had my heart since you brought those flower arrangements to my mean ass grandma," he confessed.

My face softened until I was laughing and discreetly glancing away to wipe the moisture from my eyes.

"You've been dodgin' me for years, Hood."

"You've been attached to someone more times than I can count."

"'Cause you wouldn't give me the time of fuckin' day. However, now…" He lifted his wine and prompted me to do the same. So, I did. "Now, you as good as got, baby."

Our glasses clinked. While he drank his down, it took me a minute to bring the flute to my lips to finish off my own drink.

"When we get married, that shit is forever," he added while placing his flute on the table.

"Married?" I questioned indignantly. Now he was just talking crazy.

"Married, Hood. My grandma wouldn't be pleased with me being with a woman for the rest of my life without marryin' her. That shit is tacky."

Inside my chest, my heart was leaping and flipping like I'd

drank a gallon of caffeine. Nikki wouldn't believe that her brother had finally lost his mind.

"How can I believe you, Memphis? I need reassurance." Because I'd hate to spill my feelings to him just for him to go back on his word.

He moved toward me and pushed me back until he was laying on top of me. His tasty lips met mine as he settled himself between my thighs.

"I'll give you whatever you want," he said. "Just promise me it's me and you."

I was still trying to figure out how we ended up here let alone making promises. Yet, I found myself conceding.

"Okay. It's me and you." There wasn't an ounce of fear in my declaration. In fact, I wrapped my legs around his waist to bring his stiffened dick closer to my throbbing bud. I loved that I didn't have to tell him what I wanted when it came to this. As she removed my shorts, I lifted up and spread my legs wide once he had them off.

"Ya clit is ready to explode, baby," he mumbled.

He kissed his way down my quivering stomach until his tongue lashed my hardened clit. My body bent and contorted, already on the verge of releasing the pleasure he sought. His tongue snaked inside my tunnel, fucking me while I cried his name.

"Mmm," he moaned. Memphis had his whole face in my pussy, eating me to perfection. I shrieked in ecstasy when he attached his mouth back to my clit. That quickly, I fell apart.

MEMPHIS

Pictures of me and Hood in front of the restaurant from yesterday had me grinning at the comments under the stills. The women were jealous and so were the niggas. That shit tickled me. Hood came out of the bathroom, scowling.

"Please tell them to delete it," she begged.

"I won't," I informed her with a quick smack to her ass. It jiggled and almost made me want to strip and have her before we got on the road.

"My messages are already piling up in my inbox. I can only imagine what Flo's Petals' voicemail has had to endure."

A frown covered my face. "You know what… *Now* that we are together, I'm moving you."

"Memphis, no—"

"Aht, aht, baby. Compromise."

"But that house is special to me."

"You can keep the house, Hood. Rent it out."

She pouted and crossed her arms over her breasts.

"Hood, you can't stay in that neighborhood. As much as you wanna honor ya auntie's memory, it's not safe. Especially not now. Before you were just a friend of mine. Now, you're my woman."

She smacked her teeth and rolled her eyes.

"'Less you wanna reverse and go backwards—"

"No," she hurried and said. She came right into my arms and laid her head on my chest. "Okay, I'll think about it."

"Hood."

"Give me until after Nikki's wedding," she stated. "Just let me clear my head before I make any rash decisions."

I kissed her pouty lips and acquiesced. "The day after Nikki's wedding, I want my answer."

She giggled against my chest. But I was dead ass serious.

"This is the second meeting you've cancelled this week. Everything good?"

"Of course," I told Boston. "How did ya counseling go today?"

"Nah, nigga." He chuckled. "Wassup with you and Poppi? You look stressed as fuck."

I was lowkey bothered that she hadn't pledged her love for me. Granted, I knew Hood had love for me. Her saying the words was what I needed. Now I knew just how women felt when someone they loved withheld those simple yet powerful words from them. I was going crazy.

"Do you tell Shayna you love her?"

A few seconds passed before he shrugged.

"That's fucked up," I mumbled.

He shrugged again. "You gotta mean that shit when you say it."

"Wait…you don't love ya wife? Why the fuck would you—"

"It's a long fuckin' story, bruh."

"So, I take it counseling ain't gon' help."

Again, he lifted his shoulders. "If it works, it works. Even if it doesn't, you know how my people are."

Boston's parents were ministers. They were heavily against divorce and nearly had a coronary when he married Shayna at the courthouse.

"At this point, I'm in it. Ain't shit I can do about it."

"Sounds miserable," I said. It was crazy how we worked day in and day out, and this nigga's work never suffered. We made flights, every contract, and every move together. Not once would I have thought he was going through some shit this heavy. Problems were one thing. Having your back against the wall was another thing.

"It's people who get married every day for reasons other than love. It is what you make it."

"And you're tryna make the best of it," I surmised.

He nodded. "I'ma stay loyal and do what I gotta do to make sure my wife is happy. Do I sacrifice a lot…hell yeah."

"But you can sleep at night—"

"Knowin' I did the right fuckin' thing," he finished.

I dapped him on that. "I commend you, mane. Few niggas believe in being loyal to a woman anymore."

"Is that what this is about with Poppi? 'Cause if you're thinkin' about fuckin' shit up, I'ma have to pump the brakes on that shit. There's not a woman in this world you wanted more than her. I saw it the first time she showed up to Nana McCorvey's house. She's had you ever since."

A couple hours later, Boston's words rang loud in my ears as I stood in the jewelry store paying for a pair of diamond studs for Hood. They were exquisite and would look stunning perched on her earlobes. Tonight, we were having an intimate dinner at my house. Hopefully, I could finally hear those words.

After leaving the jewelry store, I made another stop to scope out a building a few blocks over from my office. Hood wasn't sold on moving her shop, but I'd be damned if I let my woman continue to work in an area riddled with crime. Not only that, but now that she and I were together, her security was paramount. The niggas I had watching over her were doing enough for now, but that still wasn't good enough for me.

This building had more space for growth, and the security system would be top notch. In this part of town, Flo's Petals would flourish even more. Whatever I had to do to ensure Hood had anything she wanted, I was going to do.

That night, I divided my attention between Hood and the stove. She traipsed around the kitchen in nothing but a pair of black, lace panties. All her fat pussy was eating the fabric, exactly the way I wanted to.

"If you don't get off me, you gon' burn the fish." She giggled. I had her up against the island, with her ass plastered to my dick. These boxers were fighting for their life trying to contain him. Ignoring her, I took both her titties into my palms and squeezed them until she moaned. I kissed down her neck and pinched her nipples so hard she gasped.

"Can we wait to eat?" I asked while reluctantly pulling away. Turning, Hood seductively eyed me up and down, then hopped on top of the island. She parted her legs wantonly and positioned her hands behind her.

Licking my parched lips, I made quick work of removing the crispy fried fish from the cooking oil. I flipped the burner off and left her for just a second to go into the den. The box sitting on the coffee table was discreet but put a mischievous smile on my face. Going back into the kitchen, I found Hood right where I left her.

Handing her the box, I expectantly watched her open it. Just thinking about the shit I went through to get her this gift had me geeked. She ripped the box open and balked at the gift inside. The matte black replica of my dick and balls laid inside the box. Her mouth dropped as I took it from the box and carried it to the sink. As I scrubbed it clean, I smirked at every vein and ridge that I knew all too familiar.

Back between Hood's thighs, I handed it to her.

"It's me," I assured her. Her hands slightly shook as she held the object. She was still stuck on shock and inspected the dick like it wasn't something her pussy was used to by now.

"I'm away more than I like to be. The last thing I want is to neglect you."

While she stuttered over her breaths, I swallowed one of her perfectly perky globes. Her engorged nipple swelled even more as my tongue lashed at it. I removed her panties and promised to buy her more of them. They knew how to make her pussy more irresistible than it already was. I roughly tweaked the other nipple, enjoying how it made her open her legs wider. Picking them up, I pushed them all the way back until she lay across the island.

"Show me how you gon' fuck yaself while I'm away." Unabashed, she took the dick and trailed it down her abdomen until it tripped along her fat pussy lips. Slowly, she inserted it as deep as it would go, just like she liked me to do.

"Shiiittt," she moaned as her face contorted into disbelief. I parted her legs even more and licked my lips at the sight of her fat clit pulsating as she fucked herself into a nut that dripped onto the counter. Hearing and seeing how her pussy reacted to the replica of me had my dick straining for release. She pumped it in and out of herself at a pace I fucked her, too. That shit made me proud.

Dropping my head, I latched onto her nub and swiftly brought her to another nut that had her clinching the back of my head with her thighs shaking uncontrollably. Her shit was sloppy, too sloppy for me to pass up. Leaning back, I brought the dildo out of her, then stuffed my shit in all the way to the hilt.

"Fuck!" I grunted loudly. A nigga barely got my shit together before she popped my dick into her mouth and snaked her tongue around it. Watching her deep throat and suck her creamy cum off the dildo had me furiously pumping every ounce of nut I owned inside her good ass pussy.

CHAPTER 8

POPPI

Two days later...

"So, you and Memphis, huh?"

Tandy didn't even speak when she walked into my shop. She looked around like the place was foreign to her.

"Hey to you, too, Tandy."

My relationship with my sister was touch and go. Somedays, Tandy was cool. Others, she barely acted like I existed. Her wishy-washy attitude reminded me a lot of our mother's. After our aunt died, I felt like our relationship did too. Aunt Rose was the only one holding us together.

While a successful nurse in her own right, Tandy never grew to support me when it came to my flower shop. To this day, she thought it was a waste of my time and education. Although I made good money, she thought a career choice such as this was childish and beneath me.

"I must say, it surprised me to see y'all together."

In the middle of assorting an arrangement due out any minute, I didn't have time for Tandy's mood.

"Is there a question you have? Or are you just here to be negative?"

She tucked her arms one over the other and shifted her weight to one hip.

"That family is gon' chew you up and spit you out. I thought by now, you would've seen that you are not in the same league as them."

After eight years, Tandy still found it in herself to question the ways of the McCorvey family.

"Tandy, I've known Nikki and Memphis for eight years. When it comes to them, I think I'm a better judge of character than you."

One of her perfectly arched eyebrows lifted. "If that family cared about you so much, they'd move you out of the hood. Instead, here you are, in a neighborhood riddled with crime."

I wouldn't tell her how Memphis was begging me to move. Our relationship wasn't her business.

"I'm here because I wanna be here, Tandy. You were just gon' sell Aunt Rose's house like it wasn't shit to you. We grew up in this house. You saw how fuckin' hard she worked for this house."

"That was her decision. Aunt Rose had plenty of opportunity to move us out of here."

"So, what if she did!" I snapped. "We were teenagers when she took us in. Imagine having to carry the load of two girls when she had no children of her own. You should be ashamed of yourself for looking down on her. We never once went hungry or none of that shit. So, your argument that she could've done better is crazy to me."

"She slept with Mr. McCorvey. For years…"

Tandy's admission knocked the wind out of me.

"What?"

"Aunt Rose was fuckin' Mr. McCorvey. You know what he once told her. That her pussy was better than any he'd ever had and that if his wife would let him, he'd move her out of this neighborhood."

I tried recalling a time when I'd seen Memphis's father with my Aunt Rose. There was no such time to recall.

"How do you know that?" Knowing how Memphis felt about his father, I knew Tandy wasn't lying about him cheating. It was everything else that I had a hard time believing. Mrs. McCorvey was very kind to me. Over the years, she'd welcomed me into her home plenty of times. Had she known all along that my aunt was fucking her man? I wanted to throw up.

"Why do you think I told you Aunt Rose would be mad if she found out you were over there. And that they wouldn't let you step foot onto their property? You're nothing to them. At this point, it's weird as hell that they've even kept you around all these years. Especially after Aunt Rose passed."

Wiping off Tandy's remarks, I continued with my arrangement wishing she had never walked her ass up in here. Aunt Rose couldn't stand that I was best friends with Nikki, but she never tried coming in between us. Nikki and I were closer than sisters, and she never once made me feel a way that wasn't genuine love and friendship. Tandy trying to plant seeds of doubt in my mind irked my fucking nerves.

"Well, if any of that is true, at some point I would've seen it.

Aunt Rose sleeping with that man has nothing to do with me and Memphis, nor me and Nikki."

Out of the corner of my eye, I watched as Tandy shook her head in pity.

"As smart as you are, you've always been stupid."

"Bye, Tandy," I uttered. "Next time text or call before you come by."

For a minute, she just stood there watching me work. I said nothing to her, disengaging so she wouldn't say another word to me. Tandy and I had arguments often but none came to blows. In my head, I couldn't see putting my hands on my sister, no matter how much she pissed me off sometimes. I found it was better just to ignore her. She'd eventually leave.

Eventually came two minutes later. Sighing heavily, I removed my gloves and leaned over the beautiful arrangement I'd completed. Every day, life was all around me. Being around flowers brought me joy and peace that nothing in life had ever afforded me. In my shop, there was no one to talk to or listen to complain about the stresses of life. It was just me and my flowers.

That night, Memphis wasn't having my gloomy mood. He took me out to dinner at a nice restaurant by the water. He sat right next to me and kept our conversation light, observing that my energy was slightly off.

After dinner, he took me to a jewelry boutique where he added a bracelet to the beautiful diamond studs he'd purchased me. Truthfully, he spoiled me rotten, and I was letting him. Now that Tandy was in my head, I was questioning shit I had no reason to question. This was a relationship built over eight years. Falling into bed with Memphis was a beautiful thing.

Now as we walked the pier, the evening sky sparkled with what seemed like a million tiny stars. Memphis was a romantic, something I would've never discovered about him had I not taken a chance on us. He was a hand holder, a door opener, a food preparer, and a cuddler. We slept in each other's arms *every* night. Every morning, I woke up to his kisses. To say that I liked this side of him was an understatement.

And I loved him.

Dispelling Tandy's voice from my head, I plastered a genuine smile on my face and playfully grabbed my man's jawline.

"I love you, Memphis," I confessed. It stunned him so that he stopped walking and pulled me into his arms.

"I wish you'd tell me what's bothering you, baby. We promised each other that it's us. That means everything you deal with, I deal with. I'm a happier man knowing that you love me. But I'd be even happier if I knew you trusted me with anything that concerns you. I won't hurt you, Hood."

Burying my face into his chest, I prayed my admission wouldn't cause friction between us. Now that I'd professed my love, I didn't want to run him off with my doubts.

"Tandy came by today," I muttered into his black tee. Nikki was privy to me and Tandy's relationship. Memphis, not so much so. But he was aware how women worked enough to know that sometimes, they could be haters. "Did you know that your father was sleeping with my auntie?"

Memphis's body briefly tensed under my fingers. Then his fingers found my chin and lifted my face to his. He placed a sweet kiss on my lips and mumbled against them.

"I'm not my pops. He was fuckin' a lot of women. Have I

witnessed him being with ya auntie? Nah. Is it likely he was? Yeah. Does that change what's between you and me? No, the fuck it doesn't. You don't have to question how I feel about you. You don't have to question how Nikki feels about you. 'Cause one thing's for certain, we love the fuck outta Poppi Hood Bloom."

This time when he kissed my lips, he kissed away the tears sprinkling my cheeks.

"Every good thing you've ever felt about me, trust it. Trust me," he pleaded.

Hours later, Tandy's remarks were completely eradicated from my mind.

"Thank you for calling Flo's Petals, this is Poppi. How may I help you?"

Some days it was a love/hate relationship for how busy I stayed. With Nikki's wedding in two weeks, I was knee-deep in finishing up all the orders I had so that I could give all my time to Nikki's project.

"Hi, this is Tori Night. I'm told if I need exquisite flower arrangements, you're the person to call."

This woman's name and voice sounded familiar. Racking my brain, I pinpointed why I recognized her.

"Hi, Ms. Night," I replied. "Yes, I offer different types of arrangements for any occasion. Are you looking for something specific?"

"Well," she began, "I'm not sure what I'm looking for. My daughter is turning sixteen, and I wanted to make her day special. I've rented a nice banquet hall and was hoping you could come check it out and see if you can steer me in the right direction."

"Uhm...when did you need this done?"

"Her party is next weekend. I know it's short notice, but I'll make it worth it."

Tori Night was the radio host down at the local station. Doing business with her could've potentially put Flo's Petals in spaces I never thought it would be. I hated to decline, but unfortunately, I had to.

"I'm actually not available within that timeframe. I can give you another florist who may be able to assist you." I wasn't the one to gatekeep. Handing another florist business wasn't going to stop my flow.

"Listen, I will *double* whatever you want. *I* want the best and the consensus says that you're it."

She was definitely a smooth talker. Even though I wasn't hurting for money, turning down double was insane.

"How about I come take a look at the venue. If I think it's too much to get done in time, I'll be up front and let you know."

"That's wonderful! Thank you so much! The venue is White Sands North. Are you familiar with it?"

I was and that fucking place was all the way in Destin—over an hour's drive from here.

"Yes, I know the place."

"Perfect! Let's meet Tuesday...say around noon?"

"That's fine," I reluctantly agreed.

"Okay, see you then!"

I hung up and inhaled a deep breath. There was enough on my plate and adding more just seemed to be the dumbest thing to do. After Nikki's wedding, I was taking a real fucking vacation.

MEMPHIS

Finally, I was signing my name to the dotted line to acquire the Destin Tornadoes. The pro football team was building, something I wasn't afraid to do. People weren't patient enough to allow things to work themselves out. The current owner was that type of person. He didn't see the team winning in the next five years, which was cool. His impatience was nothing compared to the steadfastness that I possessed.

For months, Boston and I sat back observing college and high school games. These new kids donning cleats were just built differently. They had a tenacity that begged anyone to take notice of their talent.

As a businessman, knowing the inside and out of something you wanted was necessary. Irby Cutler, the man I sat across from, was lazy as fuck. Although a wealthy Black businessman in his own right, he wanted the money and not the work. Because of such, he was giving up a team who would, in a few seasons, be title contenders.

After I signed my part, I slid the stack of papers to Boston. Our attorneys were present, both sides exhausted from the back and forth. Lowkey, I was exhausted too. Hood had me up all night. Neither of us tapped out until the wee hours of the morning. The rest of the night I was up, wrestling with my feelings. Hood had finally confessed to loving me. Now I was wondering how soon was too soon for me to propose to her.

Chill the fuck out.

Common sense said so. However, common sense wasn't who I gave a fuck about. I wanted Hood wearing the McCorvey name like yesterday.

An hour later, Boston walked Mr. Cutler and his attorneys out as my phone rang.

"Hey, Ma," I answered. "You at the airport?"

"Hi, Son. Imagine my surprise to pull into my driveway just to find your father in the yard acting like a maniac."

My face contorted into anger.

"The fuck you mean?" I stalked out of the conference room and to my office for my keys.

"I'm not leavin' 'til you talk to me, Lenny!"

In the background, my pop's harsh, loud tone caused me to growl. All week, he'd been blowing up my phone looking for my mama. I hadn't answered the first call nor message. One thing about that nigga, he knew who the fuck to play with and who not to play with.

"Don't get all worked up. I see one of your goons across the street. I've warned him to stay back, though, and I've already called the police."

"Fuck the police!" I barked. "I'm on the way."

I hung up and hurried to the elevator. The ride to the first floor was spent with me pacing the box like a bear in a cage. As soon as the elevator opened on the first floor, I was out of it, stalking quickly to the entrance. Quell saw me rushing out of the building and followed me.

"Stay here. I'm good," I informed him. Really, I just needed to deal with my pops on my own. If Quell went, he'd have no qualms about putting a bullet in my pops.

Boston called my phone as soon as I slid behind the wheel of my truck.

"Hey, everything good?"

"Hell, naw!" I replied. "Be ready to bail me the fuck out!" I ended the call and hauled ass to my grandparents' old house. On two wheels, I slid onto the street just to see the police already there. With the truck still running, I hopped out, scanning the scenery for Jonathan. I spotted him propped against a police cruiser, trying to plead his case. He saw me coming, and his eyes widened.

Niggas killed me with the shit they did. For nearly thirty years this nigga had my mama. She was beautiful, smart, faithful, and raised his damn kids to perfection. Only for him to continuously fuck her over. Now this nigga was over here causing a scene and begging for her back like the piece of shit nigga that he was.

"Memphis, don't!" my mama shouted. She was too late and so was the cop standing there with his hands on his hips like he didn't see a fucking tornado coming.

"Bitch ass nigga!" I grabbed my pops up and beat him like he was my son.

"Let him go! Let him go!"

Guns were aimed at me, but with my pops in a headlock, it was nothing to snap his damn neck.

"Memphis!" my mama cried. "Let him go! Don't let him ruin your life!"

Blood pumped through my ears and time seemed to move in slow motion. Slowly, the slurred voices cleared. That's when I heard my pops gasping for air. My arm was banded around his neck so tightly that my veins angrily protruded. I'd never stared down the barrel of a gun. Niggas knew not to fucking try me like that. It was fucked up that it was caused by my own blood.

"Memphis, please," my mama begged.

The minute I released Jonathan, cops swarmed me. A nigga just became the owner of a football team and couldn't even enjoy my day without the bullshit.

"Earlier today, the Destin Tornadoes acquired two new owners. One half of that duo, Memphis McCorvey, was arrested less than an hour after he acquired the team. Officials say Mr. McCorvey was arrested for aggravated assault and battery, both felonies. Channel 32 has reached out to Mr. McCorvey's team for a statement on his behalf. So far, there is no other information as to who the victim was and what led to the incident..."

"The charges will be dropped by tomorrow," Nore said. He'd been my family's attorney since the first time I made a bag. Shit sometimes got sticky when dealing with the streets. Nore made sure to keep my shit together, and he wasn't above getting his hands dirty to do so.

"Are you sure?"

That was Hood. When I arrived home, she was standing in my driveway waiting for me. She ran and jumped into my arms like I had been gone for weeks instead of a few hours. Now as I sat on the sofa with her laying across my lap, I smoothed my fingers over the area where her eyes were puffy from crying.

"Absolutely. My duty is to keep him clean, and I will. At all costs. As he'll tell you, I do my job very well."

I smirked while she relaxed some.

"I'll see myself out. Gotta pay Mama a visit," he said.

My mama was all torn up over this shit. I hated to go against her, but my pops deserved every fucking bruise I left him with. No bruise was deeper than the one my mama left him with, though. That nigga cried when my mama had him trespassed from her property. Security was ordered to watch her round the clock. A man whose ego was bruised couldn't be trusted.

Hood shifted in my lap, bringing herself to straddle me. She cupped my face in her hands and softly kissed my hard-set snarl.

"You did the right thing," she whispered. "And I know a part of you hurts because of it."

"I hate my mama had to see me like that," I admitted. "She knows how I am. She's just never seen me lay a hand on my pops."

Then there was Nikki. She wanted to come over and check on me. However, Hood promised her that she had me and that I needed a minute to cool off before anyone came by. She made me a drink, cooked me dinner while I showered, and made sure I was full before she finally settled down in my lap. Everything about how Hood was handling the situation spoke to how much she loved me.

The ring was definitely already hers. I'd let Nikki have her day. Then, I was proposing to the woman I loved more than anything.

CHAPTER 9

POPPI

Not too long after I flipped my sign to open, a familiar face entered my shop. There was only one reason Daphne could be here and his name started with an M. Honestly, I was surprised she'd waited this long to pop up.

"Welcome in," I chimed to which she offered a stale smile.

From here, I could smell her expensive ass perfume. Then there was the brightness of her jewelry bouncing off her beautiful copper skin. Absently, I wondered which of the magnificent pieces Memphis bought her because my man definitely knew how to pick jewelry.

Leaving her to pretend to look around, I continued working on the arrangement set to be delivered to a woman celebrating her fifth wedding anniversary. Her husband was a new customer —one who was willing to pay whatever to make sure his wife's day was extra special. He came into the shop, skeptical at first, until he saw my work for himself.

"I was told I couldn't go wrong if I came here. I have to admit, I'm impressed."

"I've seen better," I heard Daphne mumble. She made sure I could hear her over the melodies of early nineties R&B.

"Excuse me?"

"I said I've seen better." Her gaze met mine with defiance there.

Defiance meant nothing to me. I was the queen of calm before the storm. Words meant nothing. I'd bulldoze through Daphne without even blinking. While I didn't mind getting my hands dirty, I really did hate fighting. Plus, there was the potential of losing everything I'd worked for just to dust a bitch off. I knew many Daphnes. They were the type to run their mouth and proudly take an ass whooping just to try and take you for everything you were worth. Getting beat up didn't faze women like Daphne. She was all about her money. And the fact that I had her ex meant she was out for blood.

I smirked.

"It's cute that you think this is funny."

"You're funny," I replied nonchalantly.

"What exactly do you think you have on me?"

Chuckling to tamp down the way my blood overheated, I shrugged. "I wouldn't know. You'd have to ask Memphis that question."

My response caused her to narrow her eyes at me.

"I know a lot of people. All I have to do is put in the word, and this piece of shit shop will be closed. Leave my fucking man alone."

This time, I couldn't hide the anger that soared through me.

Slamming the clipboard in my hands on the countertop, I looked her square in her unfazed light brown eyes.

"Memphis couldn't have warned you about me. Just in case you think it's sweet and try to test the waters, the current is real choppy over here, baby. Once I'm on you, a navy seal won't even be equipped to save you. So unless you ready to have your parents scrapin' you up off the concrete, I'd advise you to stay outta my shop. If *one* person comes through here on some bullshit, I'ma act like the ghetto rat you think I am and dog walk yo' tender pussy ass all the way to the cemetery. Don't let all these beautiful expressions of life make you think *anything* is cotton candy over this way."

She snickered. "As the woman carrying his baby, I wish you would threaten my life. How do you think Memphis would handle that?"

Smiling past the gag in my throat, I said, "Dunno. Let's call and ask him." I wasn't about to jump to conclusions. Especially not with a woman like Daphne. Her endgame was clear: she wanted Memphis back by any means necessary.

Promptly, I produced my phone and called Memphis right there on the spot. The phone barely rang, and I barely had it on speaker before his voice sounded.

"'Sup, my beautiful baby," he answered.

Daphne seethed at his greeting.

"Hey, baby. I apologize for interrupting your day."

"Fuck outta here," he softly chided. "You know my days ain't shit without you."

Beaming, I replied, "Hm. Well, I thought I'd let you know you're going to be a dad."

Memphis's reaction was a loud hoot. "See, Hood. I told you we were meant to be. I'm glad you listened and stopped takin' them damn pills. Lil' Memphis been waitin' to see the world."

Daphne didn't know whether to cry or scream. I, on the other hand, giggled.

"Unfortunately, I'm not the one havin' your baby, sweetheart. Daphne is."

Memphis chortled. "Bullshit! My kids ain't been nowhere but in you. She ain't even had the pleasure of swallowin' my kids. I'on trust nobody but you like that."

I busted out laughing at his crazy ass. "Memphis! That's nasty, baby. But anyway, just so you know, I wouldn't know if I was pregnant or not. It's too early. What I will say is that there's no reason for me not to be." I'd stopped my pills the first day he asked me to. That should've been a sign that I was willing to do whatever for Memphis. Not only that, but I loved him deeply.

Across the counter, Daphne's eyes steamed with hatred.

"I'm sorry… Is there anything else you needed?"

This hoe growled and stormed toward the exit. Not before knocking some of my plants over.

"Be glad you're leaving with your life, hoe!" I sang. Memphis chuckled.

"You mean to tell me you a good girl now?"

I smacked my teeth and rounded the counter to go clean up the mess Daphne made.

"Be for real. That hoe deserved to get busted in the back of her head. She may be pregnant for real, though, and I don't need those problems. Plus, I have a meeting in Destin, remember. I'm about to leave as we speak."

"Aight, baby. Be safe and call me when you pull up."

"Alright. I love you."

"I love you, too, pretty mama."

I hung up cheesing hard. Just two weeks ago, I didn't even know what Memphis's sweet kisses tasted like. Now I craved them every second of the day. Just like I craved him. In two weeks' time, I'd folded. I'd not only folded, but I was professing my love to this man.

Truth be told, I was okay with that.

"Excuse me, I'm looking for Ms. Night."

An older, brown-skinned lady with a clipboard in her hand turned around to glance at me. Her nose went up in the air as she took in my appearance.

"You came to a possible booking dressed like *that*?" she asked.

Taking inventory of what I had on, I saw nothing wrong with the black tights, black fitted tee, and black Gucci slides I had on.

"Actually," I started, "I'm not looking to be booked. I offered to meet Ms. Night here to see if what she wants is feasible for my schedule. You know…since I'm *fully* booked an' all."

"Poppi!" Ms. Night's voice sounded from behind me. She walked up to me, and air kissed me. "Thank you for coming! This is my assistant, Angela. She's here to make sure all the details are written down just in case you're able to take the job."

Right off, I wanted to decline the job off the strength of Angela. Her attitude was giving *smack me*, and I couldn't get arrested the week before Nikki's wedding. I was still wound up from Daphne bringing her dirty ass energy into my shop. Deeply exhaling, I had to shake Angela and Daphne's ass off to get this shit out of the way.

"Okay," I replied. "Let's get started."

THE HOOD FLOWER GIRL

Forty-five minutes and a whole lot of compromising later, I accepted Ms. Night's deposit. Her requests weren't too crazy, and with a little less sleep, I could get it done in no time. All next week would be dedicated to Nikki's wedding. Once I knocked both jobs out, I could take a break to just…breathe and love on my man.

Back at my shop, I sighed when I walked inside, then smiled to myself. I really turned a three-bedroom, two-bathroom house into my dream career. From the front to the back, different species of flowers and plants adorned the space that used to be the living room. The kitchen was now the room I used to create all my pieces. Two of the bedrooms doubled as extra workspace, while the room I used to sleep in was now my office. Life just didn't get better than walking in your divine calling.

Right away, I finished the last of my orders for the day, then moved into starting Ms. Night's order. She wanted a mixture of blues, her daughter's favorite color. She wasn't well-versed in what types of flowers she wanted, but I had the perfect ones. I sketched out my plans and started assembling some of the ribbon that would adorn the flowers. Thankfully, I talked her into simple and not gaudy. It would just take a couple of days to complete her order.

The bell sounded over the front door. Glancing at the wall-mounted security camera, I turned my nose up at seeing Jermaine walk through the door. Wiping my hands down my smock, I went to the front to see what it was he wanted. First Daphne and now his ass. I didn't have time for this shit. Going behind the counter, I made sure to let him know things were still as they stood between us.

"I'm just gon' cut right to the chase," he said. "What the fuck do you see in that nigga?"

"Everything," I replied with a smile.

"He's nothing but a piece of street trash who hides behind these so-called companies he has."

"If my man is street trash, then what are you? And please stop calling him names in his absence. You wouldn't say any of that to his face."

Jermaine glanced off and grit his teeth.

"I'd like for you to leave," I said. "I don't want you here…" My words trailed off as Memphis's truck slid into my parking lot. By the sound of the tires, he'd been speeding to get here.

Jermaine chuckled and shook his head. "A jealous nigga is deadly," he said.

Meanwhile, Memphis nearly snatched the door off the hinges when he walked inside. I wouldn't ask how he knew Jermaine was here. The look on his face was one of homicide, and I had to remember to breathe when he walked up to Jermaine and sized him up.

"You in the wrong hood, my boy."

Jermaine smirked. "Am I? What you gon' do about it?"

Memphis laughed, then smoothed his hand down his beard. My eyebrows lifted at the way he visibly was angry, but laughter spilled from his lips.

"I see what you tryna do. You want me to beat yo' muhfuckin' ass." Memphis was fresh off of beating his daddy's ass, so I had to swiftly step in.

"He does want you to beat his ass, baby. But you're not gon' lay a finger on him." I pulled on Memphis's arm, ushering him out of Jermaine's face.

"Get the fuck outta here and don't find ya way over here no mo'. Hood will tell you that I don't hand out chances. Take that shit and move the fuck around."

As Jermaine passed Memphis, Memphis shoulder checked him. Jermaine wanted to buck back but thought better of it. As soon as he left out of the door, I popped Memphis on his chest.

"That was too much," I half-heartedly chastised.

"Okay, but don't be hollerin' 'bout I don't reassure you. 'Cause when I reassure, it's a problem."

"Reassure with your words—"

"Actions. Words only do so much. I've never played about you. You know that."

"Right—"

"And he got a warning. Next time, I'ain gon' be too nice. He try it, he gon' get it."

Sighing, I just entered my man's arms and let him kiss me on my forehead. I wouldn't stop him. As he so sweetly put it, his way of reassuring me was his way. Beggars couldn't be choosers.

MEMPHIS

Tightly embracing my mama, I kissed her forehead and was pleased with the smile she gave. It also pleased me that she looked well rested. This shit with my pops hadn't caused her to lose any sleep. For that, I was grateful.

I waited until she took her seat back inside the booth, before sitting across from her. Nikki would beat my ass if she found out that I came out to lunch with our mama without her. Nikki was too sensitive for what we needed to talk about. Plus, Mama would open up more without Nikki present. The waitress approached and took our orders. Once she left, my mama pointedly stared at me.

"What?"

"That girl was about to dissolve into a puddle right in front of us."

My eyebrows shot up.

"You didn't see her slobbering at the mouth?"

I chuckled. "I'ain see none of that, Mama."

Her nose went up. "You okay?"

I forgot my mama wasn't into social media. If she had been, she would've seen pictures of me and Hood floating around. Then again, I was surprised Nikki hadn't said anything about us.

"Once we're done celebrating Nikki, I'm proposing to Hood."

Briefly, my mama's eyes widened before her smile grew and light entered her brown eyes. "You're finally going to follow your heart?"

Exhaling, I nodded.

"I've known all along that you were in love with Poppi." She chuckled. "Just by the way you gave her a name that only you call her. She's as tough as nails and protects Nikki like you do. You couldn't have fallen for a better woman."

I had to agree.

"She found out that Pops and her auntie—" My mama put her hand up to stop me from continuing.

"The first time your dad cheated on me, you were in the second grade. He was away on a business trip and claimed to have gotten drunk. Not once did he try and come up with a better excuse than that. It was then I knew I was no longer in love with that man."

"Ma, that was—"

"Twenty years ago—I know." She took the drink from the waitress whose eyes were on me. I ignored that shit, though, and took my drink.

"Thank you, dear. That'll be all," Mama told her. Now that she was aware Hood and I were a thing, she wasn't going to stand for any woman being in my space.

"You wasted so much time with him. Time you can't get back," I said once we were alone again.

She shook her head. "Time is what you make it, Mems."

I frowned at her calling me what people on the street referred to me as. She giggled.

"You're my son. I can call you whatever name I choose to. As I was saying, while I was no longer in love with your father, I had two children to raise. There's a certain selflessness that goes into making sure your children are happy and have stability. On both sides of your family, your grandparents have shown you what a loving two-parent household could be. I didn't want to be the failure." Her head dipped on the last line. "So, I sucked up my pride, hurt, anger…and even fear to give you and Nikki the best childhood that I could give."

I hated that for my mama. I hated that for all women who felt like staying was the only way to provide a safe and healthy life for their children. At the same time, I commended the absolute pure love they had for their children. Laying aside your own chance at life and love for your children was something most niggas knew nothing about. Instead, they could give a fuck about creating broken homes. They could give a fuck about hurt feelings and their children growing up in environments where the man was most often the best form of security. Niggas couldn't care less about shit like that.

"Do you want love to find you, Ma?"

She smirked as our food was placed in front of us. Grace was said before she continued.

"If love decides to find me, I won't be mad. If it doesn't find me, I won't be mad either. When you make sacrifices such as I did, you have to be ready for the consequences. Missing out on true love is probably a consequence that I have to own. Would I do things over? No, I wouldn't. Whatever heaven has set up for me, it'll find me."

I wouldn't lie. My mama's outlook on life did something to me. She had more heart than the man she married. Which was why a good nigga deserved her. I prayed her heart and later years wouldn't be spent alone.

"Grandma Nana would be proud of you, Mems. You exceeded anything she could've ever wanted for you." She kissed her teeth. "Hm. My son is an amazing man."

Rarely did I get emotional. Bringing up my grandma was surely to always take it there, though.

After lunch, I walked my mama outside. While standing on the curb waiting for valet, a dark-skinned nigga wearing a lab coat and funky ass smile approached. I grilled him for looking at my mama's ass. His eyes then shifted to me holding her hand.

"Lenetta?" he called, garnering my mama's attention.

At first, my mama didn't respond. She stood there with her mouth partially open, and her hand over her chest. It was as if she was looking at a ghost.

"Boris?"

It figured this nigga had a goofy ass name.

"Yeah," he proudly replied. "Why you actin' like you'on know me? Come gimme a hug, girl." He actually came closer and hugged her like I wasn't standing here. He squeezed her so tight, that she wiggled her hand from mine to hug him back. He even made a sound that turned me all the way up.

"Aye, bruh." I practically pried him off of her. "The fuck you all on my mama like that for?" Across the street, Quell looked on. I stayed him with a quick nod.

"I told you he was gon' be a handful," he said to my mama. She giggled while he laughed.

"Aye, I'on find shit funny. Who the fuck is you?" I stepped in his face, ready to knock every gray hair out of his beard if he said some crazy shit.

He pulled at his white coat, showing me the name there. "Dr. Boris Clarke. Me and Lenetta go way back."

Mama fidgeted with her short, cropped curls and cleared her throat. "We went to school together," she stated. "I thought you were in D.C."

By now valet had brought my mama's car around. She wasn't in a hurry to get in that bitch, though.

"I was until a few months ago. Moved my family back here. My kids hated leaving, but D.C. wasn't for me. The twins will be graduating high school next year."

None too discreetly, I checked for his ring. My pops was already a sorry ass nigga. I didn't need another muhfucka coming along on that dumb shit.

"I forgot. You did have children late. How's Serny, by the way?" I could tell my mama was curious. The more they talked, the more she didn't care that he was all up in her space. I stood here like I was ten instead of a grown ass nigga, bouncing my gaze between the two.

"To be honest, I wouldn't even know. We've been divorced for nearly ten years. She went her way, I went mine."

Mama swiftly eyed Boris up and down. A million questions danced in her eyes.

"So, where's that fuck nigga you married? I'on see a ring."

Now, had me and my pops been on good terms, I would've stomped a hole in this nigga for calling Jonathan a fuck nigga. But since we had something in common, I had to chuckle. Real recognized real.

Just in case that nigga Jermaine thought shit was sweet, I pulled up to the building housing the county offices and walked inside. Scanning the monitor displaying names and office locations, I quickly found Jermaine. After going through a security check, I walked right to the elevators, climbed in, and hit the button for the fourth floor.

Inside that nigga's suite, I shook my head at the starstruck receptionist sitting at the front desk.

"Mr. McCor-McCorvey. Hi!"

"I'm here to see Jermaine."

"Sure! Go right in!" She pointed to the door behind her. On it was a name plate bearing Jermaine's full name and title. Without knocking, I entered his office.

"You don't look surprised to see me," I spoke.

He shrugged his shoulders. "A weak nigga will always show his hand."

Smirking, I shut the door and watched his relaxed posture turn rigid.

"Relax... I'm a weak nigga," I taunted. "While we're here, you gon' stay the fuck away from Hood. Find you another nigga to play with that ain't as crazy as me."

He chuckled and steepled his fingers as he sized me up. Jermaine was a slick nigga who weaseled his way into local politics. Fucking with a nigga like me was going to have his ass plastered across Channel 32 news.

"Threatening an official is crazy."

"Nah, I'm definitely lookin' out for you. I hear ya mama has a weak heart. I'd hate to put her through lookin' through all ya pictures just to find the right ones for ya obituary."

He chortled to hide the sweating he'd started doing.

"*Poppi* is definitely not worth all this fuckin' energy. I cheated on her multiple times for a reason."

It would've been too easy to dive across his desk and take his head off his shoulders. Nah, with niggas like Jermaine, you had to really touch that nigga's pride...make him feel like complete shit.

"Since you wanna keep yappin', I'ma see how much bark you got when I take this fuckin' office from you."

Slowly, Jermaine's smug smile disappeared until the vein in his temple pulsed.

"Yeah... I'ma show yo' *weak ass* just how much my lady is worth."

Heading out of my soon-to-be office, I ducked my head at his receptionist. Once off the elevator, I dialed Nore.

Was I into politics? No. Was I about to stand on muthafuckin' business. Yes, the fuck I was.

"Yo," he answered.

"We 'bout to go to war," I declared.

He snickered. "With whom?"

"Jermaine Gilroy. Put my name on the fuckin' ballot."

Nore cracked up on the other end.

"You ready?" I questioned.

"Nigga, I stay ready. Let's get us a seat, my nigga."

Fuck any other deal I'd ever made. This one was going to be the sweetest.

CHAPTER 10

POPPI

"No alcohol, Poppi?"

I shook my head at Shayna. Not only did I have a migraine, but I had hella work to get back to the shop and finish. I paused just to come have brunch with Nikki. When we talked this morning, she seemed stressed the hell out. The only person I invited was Shayna because I didn't need anybody pissing me off.

"I'll have her drink for her," Nikki said. She was particularly fidgety causing my brow to furrow.

"You okay, Nikki?"

Her nervous giggle didn't fool me nor Shayna. She clocked it, and her face fell.

"Okay, okay." She pouted. "I'm scared as hell, y'all. What the fuck am I doing?"

Shayna and I were equally shocked.

"Wait, what?" Shayna's head cocked back in surprise.

"See!" Nikki whined. "Y'all think I'm crazy."

"No, we don't," I quickly informed her. Nikki was having a breakdown and going against her feelings wasn't the move. "Just talk to us and tell us what's wrong."

"Yeah, so we can help you through this," Shayna added as she hugged Nikki.

Drinks were in front of us before Nikki explained what was going on with her.

"I'm literally about to be tied to this man for the rest of my life and it scares the hell out of me." She sipped her drink as tears formed in her eyes. This shit was serious. "For years I've sat back and watched my dad hate my mama in private and love her in public. It wasn't until a few days ago that I even admitted it to myself. I thought they had the perfect marriage."

My eyes dropped to the tabletop, wondering if Memphis told her about my Aunt Rose's connection to their dad. I intended to keep that shit away from Nikki. By now, though, Mrs. McCorvey filing for divorce had made it through the circle. Plus, there was the whole Memphis getting arrested for beating up his dad. I hated that all this was happening before Nikki's wedding.

"Aw, boo." Shayna rubbed Nikki's back, then dabbed at the tears on her cheek. "I know it's easier said than done, but don't let what's going on with your parents cause you to second-guess yourself or Eddie."

My sweet tea didn't have a single kick to it to help me deal with this heaviness inside my chest.

Clearing my throat, I said, "I agree with Shayna. However, I can't say I wouldn't be feeling some type of way too. Especially with your wedding being next weekend."

"Exactly." She huffed. "But I'm not mad at my mama for

doing what she had to do. And I'm not mad that Mems put his hands on my dad either."

"What I want you to realize is that Eddie isn't your dad. You're having doubts for no reason, boo. Until Eddie gives you a reason to doubt him, don't. And just to give you some peace, Boston and I have been going to counseling lately."

That was news to me and Nikki.

"Yeah," Shayna confirmed with a chuckle. "Not for anything bad, though. We're just being intentional about our next steps. We refuse to ignore *any*thing when it comes to us. Not even the smallest shit. That's the way you need to be with Eddie. Don't be the woman who sweeps things under the rug. Before you know it, those specks will become lint piles. Handle things quickly so that the two of you are always moving forward."

"This is why you're her matron of honor," I commented, causing them both to laugh. "Marriage is no joke. It's a big step but worth it with the person you love." I reached across the table and took Nikki's hand into mine. "Nikki, you're my best friend and I pray only the best for you. You and Eddie are going to be just fine."

This time, Nikki's smile reached her eyes. As we ate brunch, I thought about Memphis and where our future was headed. Things were too new to hope for a ring. However, some part of me should've hoped that was the end goal for me when it came to him. Otherwise, I was just in another relationship hoping for the best. That feeling was depressing.

Tell him you want to move the shop.

The thought came so quickly that my heart skipped. Making such a move with Memphis had to mean something greater was coming. He wouldn't offer to move me just to let this be a normal relationship. Maybe I was tripping and just needed that drink after all. Then again, as my fingers texted Memphis, they flew across the keyboard without making the first error.

When I made it back to the shop, I was shocked to see who stood at the door pacing back and forth. I parked my car and slowly got out, wondering what the hell she was doing here. The last time I laid eyes on my mama, I was in high school.

"What are you doing here?"

My mama looked worn and strung out. Her face was gaunt and her locs matted. Yet, through all that, I saw the beauty that she used to be. Whatever caused her to lose her mind had taken so much of her life. I hated that for her.

"I came to talk to you about those McCorveys," she said.

Not her too.

"It's been over ten years since you've seen me and that's the first thing that comes out of your mouth?"

She stopped pacing to scratch her head and look at me. Her eyes shifted so much she had to be high.

"Tandy told me—"

"Wait, you've talked to Tandy?" I assumed she found out about me and Memphis some other way. Tandy hadn't once told me that she was in contact with our mother. Inside, I seethed.

"I always talk to Tandy."

Crossing my arms over my breasts only helped me calm down a little.

"She told me you and that boy were together. You can't be with him, Poppi."

"First of all, don't come on my property telling me who I can't be with. Second of all, my man's name is Memphis. Lastly, how dare you think you can just bring yo' ass over here when I haven't seen you in too many years. Only to tell me that you've been talking to Tandy. The both of you can kiss my ass."

She grimaced as if something bit her. Shoving past her, I placed the key inside my door and opened it.

"And, no, you're not welcome in here," I told her, stopping her at the door. Now I wish I would've had that fucking drink.

"Just listen, Poppi. Jonathan McCorvey is a piece of trash. Everything he stands for is garbage. Even the people who came from him."

"Don't you stand here and talk about my fuckin' family!" I hissed. "They've been more family to me than you ever will be!" I went to slam the door in her face.

"Jonathan may be Tandy's father!"

Those words were like glass crashing all around me. Snatching the door back open, I glared at my mama.

"What the fuck did you just say?"

Nervously, she fidgeted her fingers. "I said, Jonathan may be Tandy's father."

"No! Why the fuck would you say that?"

"Because!" she shouted back. "I don't know who her fuckin' daddy is! And I was fuckin' that man back then."

Leaning back, I shook my head at my mama. First my auntie and now her.

"Does Tandy know?"

"She doesn't wanna know and refuses to get the DNA test."

Because Tandy looked identical to our mother, I wasn't even sure what the hell to believe. One thing was for sure, people were really fucked up.

"Jonathan McCorvey is scum of the earth. However, every one of you women sat back and fucked with a married man, not giving a damn about his wife and children. Even if he didn't respect them, it was y'alls choice to fuck with him or not. Therefore, y'all are no better than him. Get off my property."

This time, I did slam the door in her face. Moving through my shop wasn't as carefree as it used to be. I trudged through here, half-working, and half being stuck in my head about Tandy potentially being Memphis's half-sister. Whereas I should've been almost done making the arrangements for Ms. Night's party tomorrow, I was too busy ready to burn this whole fucking place down.

MEMPHIS

"As you can see, it's move in ready. The owner has upgraded all the facilities and added central air and heating. This entire lot has exclusive parking, and this is arguably the quietest street in this part of downtown."

Not an hour after getting that text from Hood, I was standing inside the building I'd been scoping out for her.

This nigga was trying to sell me something that I'd already made up in my mind that I was buying. While I had plenty of properties under my belt, I needed something special for Hood. It was this property.

"I'll take it," I stated and motioned to Nore. "Get the papers worked out." He was working overtime for me, and I'd make sure to compensate him well for his time.

As the two men left out of the entrance, Boston whistled while his eyes scanned the open floor plan.

"I like this shit," he commented. "I'm proud of you, nigga."

"You don't think it's crazy that I'm crashin' out behind Hood?"

"Hell, nah. I wouldn't see it any other way," he said, then laughed. "That whole runnin' for office shit *is* a lil' crazy, but I can't say I wouldn't do anything differently."

"Nigga, you would've blown the office up."

Boston hunched his shoulders, then we both busted out laughing.

"Yeah, that sounds like some shit I'd do."

The door opened, with Eddie sticking his head inside. "You really just bought this shit?"

"Yeah, why?"

Eddie sighed and shook his head. He came inside the

building and looked around. "How the hell am I gon' outdo this shit? My wedding gift to Nikki is a fuckin' trip to Paris. And here yo' ass done went and bought Hood a whole fuckin' building." Plopping his hands on his hips, he shook head some more.

"Good thing my sister will love whatever you get her. Long as you treat her right, materialistic shit ain't gon' matter."

Eddie's eyes met mine, and he nodded. "Yeah, you right." We dapped on it, and for the first time, I really thought about honoring Nikki's wishes and letting him completely into the fold. After all, he was about to be my brother-in-law. Being a newly half-owner of a pro football team, and a future property appraiser, I felt like being nice.

I arrived at Flo's Petals, excited to hand Hood her keys. When I walked up to the door, the sign was set to closed, so I knocked. Seconds later, Hood appeared from the back and let me inside. Immediately, I took her face into my hands with a deep frown covering my face.

"What's wrong?" I kissed under her eyes and on her cheeks, coaxing her beautiful face to relax.

"I really don't have time to talk about it. I'm behind on a project I have to deliver by morning and the shit I'm going through is…heavy."

Removing my shirt, I kept the beater on and said, "I'm here to help. While I'm helping, I want you to tell me what the fuck is wrong, aight. We're in a relationship—one that I want us to keep strong as fuck. A part of that is being open and honest with each other no matter what the shit is and no matter how fucking heavy it is."

THE HOOD FLOWER GIRL

Hood stared at my chest, then licked her lips. "You wanna help me work?"

"While you tell me what's wrong," I added.

Sighing, she locked the front door, then led me to the back where she was working.

"Damn, this shit is beautiful, baby," I praised. One thing about Hood, her imagination when it came to flowers had always been top tier. "I've never seen so many shades of blue."

She giggled and picked up one of the flowers. "I've been dying roses for days," she said. "I'm almost at the finish line."

"I'm here to help you get there. Now tell me what to do while you explain yaself."

She pointed me to a bucket with blue dye in it and told me to get to work. I'd never dyed anything in my life, but this seemed simple enough. It was anything to help my girl. I didn't even care if I got stains on my thousand-dollar jeans. The keys even took a back seat to her concern. I'd end the night surprising her to hopefully uplift her spirits.

"Long story short, my mama came by here and all but demanded that I stay away from the McCorveys."

I grumbled hearing that shit. "It's been years since you've seen ya mama."

"Which is what I told her. The absolute audacity of her to pop up the way she did. Then she proceeds to tell me that Tandy is probably Jonathan's daughter."

"Damn, that's crazy." I chuckled.

She scoffed. "You think it's funny?"

"Naw, I don't think it's funny at all, my bloom." I dipped one rose a few times until I got it the perfect shade of blue while I gathered my damn thoughts. "Before I left for college, I was in my pops' office retrieving some money from the safe when I found a little book he kept in there. It had at least six sets of initials in it. Next to the initials were results and amounts. I memorized everything."

Knowing my pops had made other kids outside his marriage was just the icing on the cake for why I didn't respect his muthafuckin' ass. It was that day, that I completely gave up on that nigga.

"T B… I'm gon' assume that's Tandy," I explained. "And she was born in October on the 3rd."

Hood paused what she was doing to look at me. "Yes, she was. So, what did it say?"

"She ain't his. The results said negative." Shaking my head, I wished like hell I never would've found that shit.

"My mama said she doesn't know who Tandy's dad is."

I shrugged. "All my pops had to do was provide his DNA and the baby's DNA. He could've gotten Tandy's DNA without ya mama's consent. At any rate, he must've also suspected Tandy was his."

For a minute we were both quiet, until she asked, "How many does he have?"

"Four others," I answered.

She audibly gasped. "Does Nikki know? Or your mom?"

"I'm sure my mama does. It's an unspoken secret between us."

"Memphis, why keep it from Nikki? She's bound to find out at some point."

Setting the roses aside, I walked up to Hood and circled my arms around her. She lay her head on my chest and listened to me breathe.

"You ever just see something so innocent and want to protect it with everything that's in you? That's how I feel about my sister. I realize she's not a kid… But I know that shit is gon' break her heart. It's already broken just knowing my mama walked away from him. Imagine how his secrets can destroy her."

"You want her to find out on her own," she surmised. "You don't want to be the reason her heart is broken."

"I don't."

Hood's arms went around my neck, and she stood on the tips of her toes to kiss my lips.

"I love you, Memphis."

Picking her up, I carried her to a section of the counter that was clear. Her eyes sparkled when I undid the belt on my jeans. Not waiting for me, she slid out of the tights she had on and reached for me. Within seconds, I was buried between her warm thighs.

I stroked her deep, sending steady, powerful thrusts to her cervix. She clamped our lips together to keep from screaming out when I picked her up and helped her ride my dick. After the third stroke, she couldn't take it, releasing my mouth to brokenly gasp my name. Her pussy was so wet and tight, I fought for control even though she clearly had it.

Placing her back on the counter, I positioned her legs over my shoulders and went even deeper. Her broken cries and contorted facial expressions had my nut rising too quickly. Ripping the top of her smock and tee shirt, I freed her left breast, her hard nipple waiting for me to torture it.

I flicked my tongue over the hard nub, causing her to jerk in ecstasy. The vice grip she applied had me seeing double. Then she met my thrusts, her own orgasm right there. She wanted that shit bad as fuck.

"Cum on it, baby! Cum on this dick, Hood!" I hissed,

straining to hold on a minute longer. My teeth tore into my lower lip; this nut felt like straight lava inside of me.

"Memphis!" she loudly moaned. Her body bowed and took beautiful flight.

"Oh, fuck, baby!" Throwing my head back, I closed my eyes and fucked my woman so damn hard that I came, moaning her fucking name the whole time.

While I still pulsated inside her, I snatched her up by her neck and brought our faces close together.

"Thing is, I don't give a fuck what keeps comin' up. We locked in for life, Hood. A grave is the only way outta this shit. That goes for both of us. Say you understand me."

"I understand you," she replied against my lips.

Freshly showered, we returned back to work. As midnight crept up, we finished dying and arranging the roses. Just as midnight blended into a new day, I handed my baby her keys. On her office floor, atop a blanket that she kept in here, she rode my dick while I swallowed her titties. We fell asleep a little while later.

Hood jumped out of her sleep as sunlight hit her face. I'd been awake for a minute, making sure her project was just as perfect as she left it.

"Baby, you slept here without security outside. That was dangerous."

I snickered at the concern written across Hood's face. "I always got security on you, baby. Why the fuck you think don't nobody run up in here?"

"Memphis," she fussed.

"Don't 'Memphis' me. Yo' ass shouldn't be so hardheaded. And the fact that you think it's dangerous when I'm here, but not dangerous when you're here by ya damn self makes my ass itch."

She smacked her teeth, got up from the floor, and entered the bathroom.

"I'll join you for a shower," I said.

"No, the hell you won't. Sedi will be here any minute to start loading the van, and I gotta be ready to get out of here. Don't you have a contract or something to be handling?"

I really did have work to do. Like countless times in these last few weeks, I didn't mind putting work aside for her.

"I'ma stay and help you."

"Uhn, uhn. Nope. Go catch up on work, baby. It's Saturday, so your office will be nice and quiet. I've got this."

Reluctantly, I kissed her lips and let her have it. Boston was probably sick of me for being MIA anyway.

"Call me as soon as you're done. I'ma leave the office and meet you at my place. Cool?"

"Cool."

We kissed one last time before I walked out of Flo's Petals. I chucked my head at the Suburban sitting curbside. Without even being told, niggas knew where to be. The driver's side window rolled down. Quell ducked his head at me in greeting. Two of the passenger doors opened and out stepped two of the niggas whose trap was across the street. They threw their heads up. It was back to their posts for the day.

CHAPTER 11

POPPI

WHITE SANDS NORTH was a beautiful banquet hall, located just steps from the beach and perched among lavish hotels, restaurants, and shops. Even the medical offices and fast-food restaurants were stylishly built. There was money over here, and it showed.

"This is the last one," Sedi pointed out. Whenever I had deliveries such as this, I always called Sedi. He worked for another florist, who recommended him to me. Not only was he knowledgeable about caring for flowers, he was quick and had an eye for designing. With his help, setting up took half the time.

"Okay," I replied. "Thank you for your help, and I just sent your payment."

Sedi saw the incoming notification and grinned. "This is why I don't mind movin' my schedule around for you, Poppi. You always look out."

THE HOOD FLOWER GIRL

Grinning, too, I hugged Sedi and waved at him as he got in the van. Before leaving, I re-entered the banquet hall to take one last walkthrough.

A smiled graced my face as I snapped pictures of my work. I had to admit, I outdid myself. Especially on such short notice. Tori went all out for her daughter, and hopefully, her daughter would appreciate all the effort it took to put this party together.

While I appreciated my auntie and all that she did for me and Tandy, a small part of me felt bad for the girl who never had a solid relationship with her mother. If things were different, I wondered if my mama would've ever gone to this extent to bring her daughters happiness.

I wasn't one to be drawn to materialistic things. However, I couldn't lie and say a small portion of what Tori did for her daughter, any child would appreciate. For many, a simple hug from their mother would've been worth the world. Such was the case with me. I guess I never really cared to think about my mama. Not until I was in this banquet hall, listening to and observing Tori give directions to everyone she felt was half-doing their job. As for me, she simply pat me on my shoulder and smiled broadly before moving on to fuss at the next person.

Pleased with the pictures and video I created, I excused myself from the banquet hall to allow space for the rest of the decorating party to get their stuff done. My mind was stuck on my mama...and Nikki. Nikki was my best friend and holding secrets from her just felt disloyal. Especially when the information involved the woman who gave birth to me. Memphis didn't want to break Nikki's heart. Meanwhile, I didn't want to break her heart either. I feared that if Nikki found out about my mama and discovered that I knew, she'd hate me for not telling her.

"Poppi!" Tori sang, bringing my thoughts to a hard stop. "I will *definitely* be using your services again! You made this hall come to life with just *flowers*! I can't even tell you how impressed and pleased I am! Thank you!" she gushed.

That was me, bringing life to any space with the things I loved most. I loved when people appreciated flowers for their beauty and representation of life.

I beamed with pride. "You're very welcome and you know where to find me."

She air kissed me and sashayed away singing a tune. As I left out of the entrance, Angela's condescending gaze watched me.

"They're beautiful or whatever. You still need to learn how to dress and show up for a job, though."

"I still got a check, baby girl. You're dressed in a five-hundred-dollar suit and heels, yet I made more off this one job than you'll make the entire week." And that was being nice. Being disrespectful would be putting my hands on this stale, wig wearing ass bitch. I meant woman. Despite how nasty her attitude was, allowing Angela to rain on my good ass day was just immature of me. She wasn't about to mess up my bag just because she had a problem with me.

Besides, I had more pressing issues. Like talking to Nikki. All morning, the thought of her was eating me up. Before I lost the nerve, I dialed her number as I climbed behind the wheel of my car.

"Hey, boo!" she answered.

Smiling, I said, "I'm happy you sound better today, boo!"

Nikki's sigh was palpable. "I am better. You and Shayna really helped me get my mind right."

Shit... It would've been so easy to forget about what my mama and Aunt Rose did and move past this without even saying anything to Nikki. However, the longer I went without saying anything, I felt just as complicit as my blood. In fact, I held a higher standard for myself. Neither of them had a duty to be loyal to Nikki. I did.

"I know you killed the party set up," she praised. "I can't wait to see the pictures."

"I took plenty." Tori's event was broadcasted. However, she didn't want any pictures posted until after hers made their rounds. I couldn't wait for her to tag me in them. I was confident enough to know I needed to prepare for the influx of new clients.

"Are you headed back? If you're free this afternoon, I was hoping you'd go to my grandma's grave with me."

I wouldn't even ask Nikki why. Visiting Mrs. McCorvey's gravesite was always hard.

"You know I got you," I replied. Everything would be pushed aside so that I could accompany her.

"That's why I love you, Poppi. You're the only person in my life I feel like truly loves me for me." She chuckled. "I mean besides Memphis and my mama, of course. But you've always been special to me. I hope you know that."

Now more than ever, I had to come clean. It weighed on me so heavy, I closed my eyes against the prickling in them. A car's horn snapped me out of thoughts. Scanning the heavy traffic slowly moving down the four-lane street, I needed to leave this parking lot before the lunch hour traffic got any worse.

After I talked to Nikki, though.

"I love you, too, Nikki." Sighing, I just went for it. "Listen, we need to talk about something…"

My words trailed off as something across the street caught my eye. Blood rushed through my ears as I tried to make sense of what was right there before my eyes. Rapidly blinking didn't change the visual before me. Still, I observed the interaction to make sure I was seeing what the fuck I was seeing.

"Goodness...it sounds heavy. What's up?"

Getting out of my car, I held the phone to my ear and tuned Nikki out as my ears buzzed. Eyes wide, I felt moisture there and before I knew it, tears were falling.

"Nikki, I'll call you right back." Without waiting for an answer, I disconnected the call.

Time stood still as I watched one car drive away, while she floated back to her own car with a smile across her gorgeous face.

"Shayna," I mumbled. She didn't hear me because I was too far away, but my eyes definitely didn't deceive me. With fury sparking through me, I rushed across the heavily trafficked street, dodging cars trying to get to the parking lot before this bitch could escape. Shayna spotted me. Fear and guilt washed over her face as she frantically tried getting into her car.

"Poppi, wait!" she shrieked.

Poppi wait my ass! I jumped on Shayna like she was a bear, and I was a porcupine. My phone went flying and so did hers. She screamed and swung her arms trying to fight back. No words left my mouth as I beat Shayna worse than I had any other person in my life.

A visible predator was one thing. A snake was something totally different.

MEMPHIS

"You like this one?" the jeweler asked. "I can customize the set to match yours or you can do something a little more timeless."

"Nah, I definitely like this one." Hood would love the square cut diamond ring with its dainty band. It was perfect for her dainty ring finger.

"How soon can you have it done?"

"Give me two weeks."

"Perfect," I responded.

After leaving the jewelers, I went straight to the office to try and knock out some work before Hood was done. Tonight, I wanted to shower her with congratulatory gifts for being the bad ass woman that she was. One thing I would continue to do was uplift my woman. I would take every opportunity to remind her how bomb she was and that I was honored to have her in my life.

"I thought you changed ya mind," Boston quipped when I walked into the business suite we owned. It compassed one half of the floor, and within the next year, we planned to buy the entire building. Now that we owned a football team, our staff would be growing and need space. Where it was once just me, Boston, and our assistants, we'd be adding additional staff to keep McCorvey & Kelly operating at its highest potential.

"Just had to make a quick stop," I replied. I entered my office, made myself comfortable behind my desk, and dove into something not as satisfying as Hood. Nothing satisfied me like she did.

By noon, I was aggravated as fuck.

Me: Wya, baby?

I followed the text up with another phone call. Hood should've been back in the city by now. Then, I felt crazy for blowing her up. If something was wrong, Quell would've called me by now. The feeling in the pit of my stomach didn't calm down, no matter how much I told myself that she was working. Which is what I was supposed to be doing.

Everything in my life centered around Hood, though. I could spend every second with her and still crave more of her time. Falling in love with the only crush I ever had, had to be meant. Everything I felt for her was soul deep, from the way she was passionate about flowers to the way she was passionate about me.

Honestly, I was blessed. Not many people could say they actually captured the person they truly loved. Settling was so normal in society that I hardly thought anyone cared about shit like soulmates anymore. However, now that I had mine, there wasn't a person in this world who could convince me that soulmates didn't exist.

For a nigga like me, owning my feelings wasn't complicated. My grandma taught me that shit. At an early age, she taught her grandchildren that it was okay to express our emotions. While I held mine at bay in the street world, in my world with Hood, I had no problems expressing how I felt about her. She stayed on my mind more than anything.

After another twenty minutes passed without a call back or reply, I stood and moved from behind my desk as an uneasiness I couldn't explain settled over me.

"You good?" Boston stuck his head in my door just as I dialed Quell's number. His shit went straight to voicemail, causing my face to screw up.

"Hell, nah. Something's wrong with Hood." Even to my own ears, I sounded worried.

"Quell is with her, right?"

I nodded and tried Quell's number again. This time it rang. As it continued to voicemail, I growled.

"The fuck." Concerned now, Boston produced his own phone. "I'ma call that nigga," he said. Only his call went to voicemail, too.

Fret seized me like no other. "I'm heading over to where she's supposed to be at." I pinged her location and confirmed her phone was still in the location she was setting up at. While that should've given me some comfort, it didn't.

"I'll ride witchu."

Work was forgotten; Boston and I headed out of our office and into the hallway toward the elevators. It was eerily quiet on the floor as there was no one here except me, Boston, and the building's cleaning crew. As we stepped on the elevator, my phone trilled. Seeing Quell's name come up on my phone screen, I answered it already on high alert.

Placing the phone on speaker, I barked, "Aye! Why the fuck ain't nobody answerin' my fuckin' calls?" In an instant, I went from being worried to being angry.

"Bruh, ya girl just got arrested," Quell spoke the same time as me. His voice sounded out of breath.

"What?" My roar of disbelief shook the elevator as it dinged on the first floor. I was out of that bitch and stalking to the entrance like whatever cop who put handcuffs on my woman was standing just outside the doors where I could strangle their muthafuckin' ass.

"Mane, I'on even know what the fuck happened. One minute she was sittin' in her car, the next she was flyin' 'cross the fuckin' street like a bat outta hell. She jumped on Shayna and Mika. She was hollerin' 'bout Shayna fuckin' Eddie or some shit."

The building could've been falling down around us. That's how fucking loud Boston growled. He tried snatching my phone away, but both of us were like tigers set loose in the wild.

"The fuck you mean, nigga?" I raged. Eddie was fucking around on my sister. Better yet, that nigga was fucking around with my day one's bitch.

"I told you I'on know what happened. I didn't see shit but Poppi runnin' her ass 'cross that damn street. By the time I got to her, she was already fuckin' both of them up."

"Where the fuck you at?" By now, Boston and I were outside. He stalked angrily toward his own ride, while I high stepped it to my truck. I dove inside and took off. Boston skid out of the parking lot, undoubtedly on his way to find Eddie… and Shayna.

"Nigga, I've been sittin' in the back of a fuckin' opps car tryna get to my fuckin' phone. I tried breakin' the fight up, but Poppi's ass started swingin' on me, so the opps thought I was involved."

Fuck! "I got you, my nigga."

"Naw, I'm good, bruh. You need to get to the county and see 'bout Poppi. She fucked them bitches up pretty bad."

"I 'preciate you for lookin' out. I'm on the way to her."

"Bet."

I disconnected the call just as I hopped on the interstate. Nore was my next call.

"Say less," was all he said. There wasn't a doubt in my mind that he would handle this shit.

The drive was going to take a minute and as much as I was worried about Hood, Boston and Nikki crossed my mind too. I would have to deal with Nikki in person. Boston…I had to get him on the line to try and talk him into handling Eddie as quietly as possible. Because I knew there was no way he was going to let that nigga live.

We had so much riding, though. Letting a nigga like Eddie and a bitch like Shayna ruin that shit was like handing them our future. I wasn't sure what Mika's role was. However, if Poppi put her hands on Mika, that meant that damn girl knew. As much as all three of them deserved to wake up on the other side, Boston and I fought to hard for this life we had. We sacrificed too much just to let some snake muthafuckas rip anything from us.

"What?" he answered. This nigga sounded too calm which was definitely not a good sign. I knew how to deal with rowdy Boston. Calm Boston was the type to take himself to hell just to chop it up with the demons.

"I'm on the same shit you on," I said. "At the same time, though, you the same nigga who told me you don't even tell ya wife you love her. I understand you gon' do what you gotta do, and I won't blame you for it. But ask yaself if takin' this nigga's life is worth it."

Boston hung up on me, letting me know exactly where his head was at. Stuck between going after him and rushing to get to my woman, I decided Eddie had made his own fucking bed.

I had to get to Hood.

A little over an hour later, I arrived at the county jail. It took no time to post Poppi's bail and get her the fuck out of here.

"I'm so sorry, baby." She came into my open arms, sorrow written all across her face. I picked her up and carried her to the truck, kissing all over her face in the process. She'd been crying and her face was full of stress.

Placing her inside my truck, I buckled her seatbelt and kissed her lips again. Once I was inside the truck, I sped out of the parking lot. Poppi sniffled, prompting me to reach for her. She undid her seatbelt, lifted up the center console, and leaned her body into me. I placed my hand on her thigh, while she laid her head on my shoulder.

"Everything's gon' be aight, my baby. As long as I'm on this earth, I'm gon' always protect you."

She snuggled deeper into my body, clinging to me like she trusted every word I said. I meant every word I said.

"I love you."

"I love you, too," she echoed. "My heart breaks for Nikki," she muttered seconds later.

So did mine. My sister was the most innocent woman I knew. All I've ever wanted to do was protect her from niggas like Jonathan McCorvey. Only for a nigga like Eddie to wiggle his way in and threaten my sister's happiness and peace.

"Nikki's gon' be aight, too."

If Boston had anything to do with it, Nikki was going to be just fine.